Bell Buckle
Biscuits

Bell Buckle Biscuits

Stories by
Margaret Britton Vaughn
Poet Laureate of Tennessee

Edited by
Carole Knuth, Ph.D.

Margaret Britton Vaughn

Bell Buckle Press
Bell Buckle, Tennessee

Library of Congress Cataloging-in-Publication Data

Vaughn, Margaret Britton, 1938-
    Bell Buckle Biscuits: stories / by Margaret Britton Vaughn.
        p. cm.
    ISBN 1-882845-07-2
        1. Bell Buckle (Tenn.) – Fiction. 2. Southern states –
    Fiction. I. Title.

PS3572.A94 B45 1999
813'.54–dc21

                                                    99-047388

2nd Printing

Printed by Lewisburg Printing
Typesetting by Brenda Brothers
Cover by Bob Clanton

For information address: Bell Buckle Press, P.O. Box 486, Bell
Buckle, TN 37020.

To
Friends in Bell Buckle,
A Town Full of Originals

Other Books By
Margaret Britton Vaughn

The Light In The Kitchen Window

Kin

Grand Ole Saturday Nights

Acres That Grow Stones

Life's Down To Old Women's Shoes

TABLE OF CONTENTS

Bell Buckle Biscuits

Beulah Atkins was famous for her homemade biscuits. Through the years, everyone in Bell Buckle had eaten them. Most folks had eaten them in school since Beulah had worked in the school kitchen for fifty-two years, and when she wasn't cooking in the cafeteria, she was rolling out her homemade biscuits for church socials and community suppers. No funeral was held in Bell Buckle without Beulah taking biscuits to a home or the funeral parlor.

Beulah sure understood funerals. Her mother died when she was in the seventh grade, and Beulah quit school to help her daddy raise her younger brother and three sisters. Some people think Beulah married so young because she needed help in the raising of her own family. Another man brought into the home would help with the chores and with the raising of her sisters and brother. Beulah was only fifteen, but she grew up in a hurry. The death of her mother and a wedding band at such an early age rounded off any playful years that she would have known. Within five years of being married, Beulah's husband, Ora, was killed in a tractor accident when he was pulling logs and the tractor reared up, throwing him under one of the large wheels. Beulah was left with her family and a nineteen-month-old daughter of her own, so she was no stranger to hardships. Her siblings relied on her even after they were grown. It just seemed they always needed a mama, and Beulah was the stand-in. Making biscuits became her way of life. She fed the whole town biscuits: her own family, then everybody else's family that got their education in the small Bell Buckle schoolhouse. When it came down to it, Beulah was everybody's mama and in later years, grandmama to the community. Beulah used to laugh and tell everyone, "Lord, I've rolled out enough dough to cover the whole state of Tennessee." And she had blue ribbons to show for her efforts. She'd won about every county fair in her small town

9

and in all the communities around, but the blue ribbons didn't mean as much to Beulah as the satisfaction of hometown people loving the taste of her creations.

Beulah raised her family like she was baking biscuits. The flour was the foundation to build together beliefs and values of small-town America. The buttermilk gave the foundation paste to bind the family together through thick and thin and be there for each other at all times. The baking powder made the biscuits rise against all odds; a family, too, had to be raised against all kinds of odds so that the troubles of life would not weigh down the joy of living. It was the lard that gave spirit and caused the biscuits to spread out. Beulah gave her family space but knew they all had common ground. A pinch of salt gave the extra flavor so life would not be boring. However, the ingredients were just part of the biscuit making and family raising. The shaping of dough was as important as the ingredients. The biscuit board was the ground that gave the foundation the strength to stand on its own, and the sharp-edged empty Pet Milk can, with a hole on top to reduce pressure, cut out the bitterness and gave a round edge to life, but it was the hot oven that brought it all together. Life came in all degrees, and it was the heat that caused the magic to come full circle. Beulah herself had come full circle; she had lived her life by the recipe and now she was facing the last ingredient: death. She hadn't counted on cancer. That wasn't in her cookbook of life, but in a good book one never knows the ending. Now, at seventy-nine, she lay in a hospital bed reading her last chapter. As friends came by to visit her, together they turned back pages through the years and talked of bygone days. Though Beulah was in pain, she still wanted to see old friends and family. They had been there from the beginning, and she wanted them there for the end. Beulah had just drifted off to sleep when the bed was jarred and she awakened to hear Frances Coleman apologizing.

"I'm sorry I woke you; I know you need your sleep."

"Shucks, Frances, I got time to sleep when they put me in the ground."

"Now, Beulah, don't go to talking about dying; you're not going to leave us anytime soon." Frances turned her head toward the landscape picture on the wall.

"There you go, Frances; no tears, honey, we've had enough through the years."

Frances looked back toward the bed, as if Beulah had struck a memory. "Lord, Beulah, you remember the day I got news about my boy dying in the war? He died so far from home and so young. You came over with food and your biscuits; Lord, he loved your biscuits. We cried together, and you stayed beside me all night. I still ain't over it. You raise a child, and then God calls him home at such an early age." Beulah squeezed Frances' hand. "You ain't supposed to outlive your children, Beulah. Listen to me go on about me; I'm here about you. Is there anything I can do for you? Check on your house or something? Lord, it just seems like yesterday when your Caroline was just a youngun; now she's all grown up with a daughter of her own."

Frances and Beulah talked on until a nurse came in with lunch. Meals in the hospital were never as good as the ones at home, but Beulah didn't really care. The chemotherapy had left her weak, and she was losing weight rapidly. She managed to eat a spoonful of carrots and mashed potatoes, then drift off toward sleep. But sleep wasn't in the cards for Beulah. Like Rook that she played through the years, Beulah was the widow and someone was always bidding for her time. Now time was running out and everybody was dropping by, but this was the way she wanted it.

John Pickens and his wife Cora gently knocked on the door, and Beulah smiled and buzzed the nurse to pick up her leftover lunch.

"You didn't eat very much, Beulah," said Cora. Beulah motioned for them to sit. Cora sat down by the bed and John pulled up a chair that was by the window.

John, dragging the chair, said, "It's a pretty day, Beulah; want me to open the blinds a little?"

"A little, John. The glare hurts my eyes if they're opened too much; besides, I don't want you to see how awful I look."

"Now, Beulah, you look plum pretty," said John.

"I know better than that, John Pickens! Most of my hair has fallen out, and I don't weigh as much as a tow sack full of cotton."

"Well, you look just fine, and you'll be putting that weight back on in no time, just you see."

Beulah smiled and noticed the dress Cora had on. "That sure is a pretty dress, Cora."

Cora touched the lace and said, "This old thing? Why, I've had it for years. I bought it that Easter you made those eggs for everyone in school. They were the prettiest Easter eggs I've ever seen. You must have been up for days getting all those names on them."

Beulah reminded Cora how Billy Atkins and Bobby Smotherman had rolled their eggs down the hall, and Bessie Tidwell slipped on one and nearly broke her hip. Cora laughed and reminded Beulah that Bessie was so fat that she would have had a hard time breaking anything with all that cushion.

Beulah hadn't taken her eyes off Cora's dress. "Cora, are you really attached to that dress?"

"Goodness, no, do you want to borrow it?"

"I want to be buried in it." Cora looked stunned. John jumped up and asked Beulah if she was sure she didn't want the blinds opened more.

Cora reached over and touched Beulah's arm. "Beulah, you know you can have this dress, but let's not talk of a burying dress. Goodness."

"I've made my plans, Cora. Gonna have my service in the First Baptist Church and be buried next to Ora and Papa. I've paid for my headstone and burying–just hadn't picked out my dress–and Cora, I hate to say this, but that dress will look better on me than you."

"Beulah, you always had a sense of humor, even when times were bad. I'll get this dress cleaned and take it over to your house, but I don't want you in it for a long, long time."

For several weeks, people stopped by the hospital. Beulah returned to her home for a short while, and people continued to drop by and talk about old times. A lot of the old times had been forgotten though Beulah's mind remained good. It was just hard for her to know what other people had remembered.

The short while at home gave Beulah time to reflect on her life. She had kept the house she was born in. Her papa had gone on years before, and her sisters and brother had places of their own. Beulah worried about her daffodils. Who would take care of them? They had been planted years ago by boys who attended the small Webb School started by Sawney Webb. Beulah knew Sawney and his son Will, and had even taken a boy to board a few times. In early Webb years, there were no dormitories, and boys boarded in homes in Bell Buckle. Beulah had pictures of the boys and wondered what happened to them. Now and then one would stop by and say hello, but they had scattered in all directions like seeds in the wind. But the daffodils always reminded her of them.

She knew she was dying, and though people prayed, she always said, "Pray for the young. I've lived my life, and though God hears every prayer, He might not have time for all to be answered, so don't waste one on me. Give it to someone who really needs it."

And like the prayers, Beulah made arrangements to give her belongings to those who needed them. She taped names to backs and tops of furniture. She wanted her bedroom suite to go to her granddaughter. She would need it. She was just starting out on her own. The bedroom suite had belonged to her mother and father, and she wanted to keep it in the family. However, there were pieces that didn't have family ties, so Beulah taped them with names of families she thought would want a table or chair and other things. She wanted her daughter to have the quilt that her grandmama had made. Beulah had slept under it for years. The flower garden pattern reminded her of the daffodils and roses planted along her sidewalk. She was leaving the house to her daughter. Houses were going for a lot of money in Bell Buckle and with people moving to the small town in large numbers, Beulah knew that her daughter could get good money for the old house since that's the kind people were really looking for now: houses made with good seasoned lumber and made to stand through the years. But Beulah wanted to be buried with the broach that Ora had given her on their wedding day. Several people thought Beulah should leave the broach to her daughter, but Beulah wanted to take one thing that was hers.

Months went by, and Beulah was going down fast. She was back in the hospital, and this time she knew she would not come out. Friends continued to stop by, but they stayed in the hall so as not to disturb her. Family members would take turns sitting beside her bed.

Most of the time, Beulah was semi-conscious. By now, Caroline and her daughter Emma were sitting day and night with Beulah. Late one afternoon, Beulah awoke while Caroline was pouring Jergens lotion into her mother's hands.

"This buttermilk needs more flour," said Beulah.

Caroline reached over and shook talcum powder into the lotion. Then she placed her own hands in her mother's wet ones.

Beulah began to caress her daughter's fingers. "We've got to show Emma how to make biscuits. Don't knead too much, Emma; it will spoil the dough and make the biscuits hard."

Beulah continued to work Caroline's hands. "Need more grease; this dough is too dry."

Caroline removed the lid of a small jar and scooped out two fingers of Vaseline.

"Emma, I taught your mama how to make biscuits and she

turned out all right. Remember that it's the ingredients. I need to roll these out. Hand me my biscuit board."

Caroline picked up the *Life* magazine that some family member had been reading and placed it on her mama's lap.

"Here, Mama, you can roll them out on this." Caroline handed her mother a glass, and Beulah patted Caroline's hands and began to roll the glass on them.

"Now, you've got to cut them round and never let pressure build up; always leave an opening."

Caroline reached over and got the Vaseline jar lid, and Beulah began making small circular indentations on Caroline's flat hands.

"Raise your children on biscuits, Emma. They're a guide for living. I hope these I just made will turn out all right."

A few moments later, Beulah breathed her last. With tears in her eyes, Caroline handed the *Life* magazine to Emma and then went home to get Ora's broach and Cora's dress.

Bell Buckle Biscuits

The Baptizing of Jo Jo Jessup

Buck Ladner and Herschel Pate sat on the back pew of the Mt. Zion Baptist Church. It was the annual summer revival meeting in the country church, and Buck and Herschel felt obliged to support the week-long meeting with their presence. Of course, the main reason they were there was it got them out of plowing the fields for a week. Any time there was a choice between Jesus Christ and John Deere, Jesus Christ won every time.

They never heard much of any of the sermons since most of their hour was spent opening up the hymnbooks simultaneously and reading the song titles from left to right. It was always an amusing pastime being able to read "Will There Be Any Stars in My Crown?" followed by "No, Not One."

However, at this particular morning meeting, the Reverend Stegall raised his voice about as high as he raised his Bible. And every time Buck and Herschel looked up, Reverend Stegall was watching them. His old, gray, raised eyebrows almost gave his old bald head a new set of hair.

Buck and Herschel had just amused themselves by opening their hymnbooks to "In the Garden" and "My Feet Are Planted on Higher Ground."

"Repent!" yelled Reverend Stegall as he slammed his fist on the shaky old pulpit.

Buck and Herschel nearly jumped out of their overalls. "We better put these hymnbooks away. He's looking right at us," said Herschel.

"What we got to repent about? We ain't done nothing," said Buck.

"I said repent, be baptized and be saved," yelled the Reverend.

"No one has joined this church in six months. This congregation is failing in its duty to bring lost souls to the Lord. Lost souls, do you hear me? The Lord said the shepherd cannot sleep until all the sheep are accounted for."

The Reverend pulled out a white handkerchief and wiped his sweaty brow.

Buck nudged Herschel. "Time for him to be taking off his coat. He always works himself up when he gets to talking about the sheep."

"The Shepherd is coming again and there are lost sheep wandering around drinking poison, cussing, and running around on loved ones. It's up to us to bring them back to the fold. We got to lead them sheep down to the river and up to the Lord. We got to baptize them sheep."

Buck nudged Herschel. "Has he ever smelt wet wool?" Reverend Stegall pointed a finger at Buck. His patience with the two had about run out.

"What did you say, son? If you got something to say, you say it to the whole congregation."

Buck jumped up and yelled, "I know a sheep I'm bringing to the Lord."

Herschel pulled at Buck's britches. "Sit down, Buck. What's the matter with you?"

The Reverend smiled. "Well, son, if you know a lost sheep, then we'll wind this service up, and we'll meet you by Buttercup Creek this afternoon. You bring your sheep and there'll be a great baptizing and a soul will be saved."

Reverend Stegall called on Leonard Hunt to dismiss the congregation in prayer. Herschel never closed his eyes during the dismissal prayer. All he could do was look straight ahead and think what Buck had got them into.

Reverend Stegall stood in the doorway of the old church shaking hands as the congregation left the service. Herschel and Buck slipped out through the crowd.

"Buck, has all that sheep talk made you crazy? Who do we know we can get baptized?"

Buck squinted his eyes as they walked in the noonday sun. "Jo Jo," he answered.

18

"Jo Jo!" Herschel raised his voice. "Did you say Jo Jo? Why the only time he's ever come to church was when his grandmama died and when the outhouse caught on fire."

Buck looked at Herschel. "Lord, Herschel, you ain't told nobody about us smoking in the outhouse have you?"

"Are you kidding? My paw would bust my britches if he knew we caused the fire. Lord, you've done it now, Buck. Why, Jo Jo is one brick short of a load. He's fifteen and in the seventh grade with us. How you gonna get him to church when they can hardly get him to school? How we gonna talk Jo Jo into getting baptized?" asked Herschel.

Buck stuck his hands into his overall pockets, kicked a rock down the dusty road where he was walking and said, "Scare him."

"What do you mean, scare him? Jo Jo ain't scared of nobody."

Buck cut his eyes over to Herschel and said, "He's scared of the Devil."

"Scared of the Devil? Jo Jo is a devil himself. His own mama owned up to that."

"I gotta good plan."

Herschel scratched his head, squared off, looked Buck right in the eye and said, "What is it?"

"Herschel, you remember what we studied in history last week?"

"Naw."

"Oh, you remember, Herschel, about the plague. All them people dying. Had something to do with butter. I think it was called Bluebonnet. You remember. We studied it last week."

"Yeah, I recollect something about it. I just didn't pay much attention to it."

Buck reached up and put his arm around Herschel and said, "Pay attention now, Herschel, 'cause that's how we're gonna get Jo Jo baptized."

"What you talking about, Buck?"

"We're gonna scare Jo Jo, Herschel. We're gonna scare him into getting baptized."

"Just how we gonna do that, Buck?"

"We're gonna convince Jo Jo that the plague is on its way to Bell Buckle and he might die of it. And if he ain't baptized, he's going straight to Hell."

Shaking his head, Herschel said, "Jo Jo don't care if he goes to Hell or not. Like I told you, he ain't scared of nothing."

"Yeah, he is, Herschel. Everybody's scared of going to Hell. They may not admit it, but when they get near death, they're scared!"

Herschel and Buck saw Jo Jo sitting on the fence down the road eating a Sunday morning biscuit. "There he is, Herschel. You stay cool. This is gonna work."

Buck walked up to Jo Jo. "What you doing, Jo Jo?"

"Aw, just sitting here spitting. What you boys up to?"

"We've been to church," said Herschel.

"Ain't y'all got nothing better to do?"

Buck looked over to Herschel and said, "Reckon we could spend our mornings sitting around spitting with Jo Jo."

Herschel looked over at the Campbell's Chicken Noodle Soup can Jo Jo was aiming at. "Yeah, we can't hit that can like Jo Jo. That takes special learning."

Buck turned and looked out across the field and said, "Reckon when it's gonna get here, Herschel?"

"I speck around Wednesday," said Herschel.

Jo Jo looked at Buck and Herschel. "What's gonna get here? What you boys talking about?"

Buck looked over to Herschel and said, "Ain't no reason to worry Jo Jo with it, Herschel."

"What you boys talking about?"

"Oh, it ain't nothing," said Buck.

Jo Jo reached up and scratched his head.

Buck noticed Jo Jo's movement. "What's that you just done,

Jo Jo, just then when you put your hand on your head?"

"I ain't done nothing but scratch my head."

"That's the way it starts, ain't it, Herschel?"

"What starts?" asked Jo Jo.

"Like you said, Buck, ain't no sense causing Jo Jo no worry."

"What the hell you boys talking about?"

"Oh me, Buck. We've gone and done it now!"

"Gone and done what?" said Jo Jo.

Herschel shook his head. "Whoo-oo, we're in trouble now."

Jo Jo jumped down off the fence. Buck looked over at Herschel and said, "Well, Jo Jo's strong. I reckon he'll make it."

"If you boys don't tell me what you're talking about," said Jo Jo, "I ain't gonna let you borrow my buck knife."

"You wouldn't do that to us, Jo Jo," said Herschel. "After all, we're just trying to help."

"Help what?" asked Jo Jo. "What you talking about?"

"Well, Jo Jo," said Buck. "You got to promise you won't tell nobody. Ain't that right, Herschel? He can't tell nobody."

"That's right, Buck. Jo Jo, you got to promise. You can't tell nobody, 'cause we got to keep it from all the women and children."

"I promise. Now what is it?"

Buck walked up a little closer to Jo Jo and said, "It's the Bluebonnet."

"What's Bluebonnet?" asked Jo Jo.

"It's coming here," said Buck.

Herschel looked over to Buck and said, "Now there's no reason to alarm Jo Jo, Buck; after all, he just scratched his head. That's just one of the signs."

"Are you boys crazy? I scratch my head all the time."

"Yeah, but think back, Jo Jo. Was it itching like it always does, or was there something different about this itch?"

Jo Jo looked over at Buck and Herschel. "You boys ain't making yourselves clear about what you're talking about."

"Well, Jo Jo, now you promise you won't tell nobody?"

"Cross my heart and hope to die."

"Don't say die, Jo Jo," said Buck. "Don't even be thinking that way."

"Well, get on with it. What you got to tell me?"

"It's the Bluebonnet," said Buck. "It's on its way, and like Herschel said, it oughta be here by Wednesday."

"What's the Bluebonnet?" said Jo Jo. "You boys talking in riddles."

"It's the plague, Jo Jo," said Buck. "That's why they're keeping it from the women and children. It's just awful! People everywhere are gonna die. Have you been saved, Jo Jo?" asked Buck.

Buck looked over at Herschel and winked. "Aw, like you said, Herschel, there ain't no sense in alarming Jo Jo now. He's just got the first sign."

"Ya'll tell me more about this here plague."

"Aw, Jo Jo, you don't want to hear any more about it. It's awful. First it starts by scratching your head, then your eyes glass over...kinda like yours, Jo Jo."

Herschel tapped Buck on the shoulder. "There you go alarming Jo Jo. He probably ain't getting it. I mean, after all, scratchin' your head and glassed over eyes are just two of the signs."

"I know he ain't getting it, Herschel. It ain't even s'pose to be here before Wednesday."

Jo Jo nervously looked at Buck. "Where is it now, Buck?"

"It's over in Bucksnort. They've had to put beds in the hospital halls. People screaming and dying with it. It's just awful, Jo Jo. First it starts with scratching your head, then with your eyes getting glassy; then, you break out in big sores, big as your mama's biscuits. What's that you scratching on your arm, Jo Jo?"

Jo Jo looked down at his arm. "A skeeter bite."

"Lord, thank goodness for that!" Buck said, looking over at Herschel. "Just a skeeter made that sore. You ain't got nothing to worry about, Jo Jo."

Jo Jo ran his hand in his pocket, took out a handkerchief, and wiped his forehead. "Tell me more about these people dying."

"They're all dying, Jo Jo," said Buck, "young and old alike. It ain't sparing nobody."

"Nobody?" said Jo Jo.

"Nobody, Jo Jo."

Jo Jo got up real close in Buck's face. "Look in my eyes again, Buck. Do they still look glassy?"

"I told you, you don't have anything to worry about. Lots of things cause glassy eyes, and, like you say, that sore on your arm's just a skeeter bite. I mean just 'cause you're the first person I've seen this year that's seen a danged skeeter, that ain't no reason to believe one didn't bite you. Herschel, have you seen any skeeters this year?"

"Ain't seen a one, Buck."

"Well, what was that you and Buck was swatting at when I saw you coming down the road?"

"Honeybees. We were swatting honeybees, weren't we, Herschel?"

"Well, maybe that's what bit me."

"Don't look like no honeybee sting to me, Jo Jo. Look, Herschel, what's that look like on Jo Jo's arm?"

"Looks like a sore to me, Buck."

All of a sudden, Buck jumped back and yelled. "Good God, Jo Jo, don't look toward the sun. It's reflecting somethin' awful in your eyes."

"Now, Buck, there you go scaring Jo Jo again. Just 'cause the sun's reflecting off of Jo Jo's glassy eyes don't mean nothing."

"I got it, ain't I, boys? I got it," yelled Jo Jo. "What can I do? Oh, God, give me a shot or something."

Buck put his hand on Jo Jo's shoulder. "There ain't no shot. It just hits you and you're gone."

"What can I do, Buck? I don't wanna die."

"Like I said, Jo Jo, there ain't nothing you can do once you got it, but there's one thing you can do that can help you later on."

"What's that, Buck?"

"Saved, Jo Jo. You've got to be saved!"

"Saved?" yelled Jo Jo. "Saved from what?"

"Hell."

"Hell? What the hell you talking about? Here I am dyin' of some plague, wanting to be saved from that, and you're talking about Hell."

"Tell him, Herschel. Tell him that if he thinks dying of the plague is something, he ain't seen nothing until he hits Hell."

"That's right, Jo Jo. It's burning forever in a lake of fire. At least, with the plague, you just scream for a while before you die. In Hell, you scream forever and forever."

"What makes you think I'm going to Hell?"

"You ain't been baptized. You got to be baptized to escape Hell. Lord, Jo Jo, we're just trying to help. We don't want you going down there."

"Well, what if I don't get it? You said you might be mistaken."

"You might not got it. Just 'cause you're scratching your head, your eyes have turned glassy, and you got a big old sore don't mean you got the plague. You might have the Tommyrot."

"Tommyrot!" shouted Jo Jo. "What's that?"

"Tell him, Herschel."

"Lord, Jo Jo, pray you got the plague. Tommyrot's the worst thing that can happen to you."

"That's right, Jo Jo, listen to Herschel. It's the worst thing that can happen to you, except going to Hell. But you might have a chance. Brother Stegall preaches all the time about how, if you got faith, you can do anything–like make yourself well. But you got to be baptized to have faith. And if the faith don't work, and you die, you still got baptized, so you don't go to Hell," said Buck.

"You mean to tell me that going down to that river might make me well, and I ain't going to Hell if I let the preacher dunk me?"

"That's right, Jo Jo, and we ain't got much time. Maybe since you just started scratchin' you might got time. Run to Brother Stegall, Herschel. Tell him to meet us at the river. Jo Jo's gonna be baptized and saved!"

Before Jo Jo could say anything, Herschel took off running down the road toward Brother Stegall's house.

"Come on, I'll help you to the river." Jo Jo put his arms around Buck's shoulders.

"Put your weight on me." Jo Jo leaned on Buck. His face had turned pale.

"You ain't gonna throw up, are you, Jo Jo?"

"I'm so sick I don't know if I can make it to the river."

"You can make it. You gotta make it. Wanna stop and rest awhile in the shade?" Buck pulled Jo Jo toward a big oak tree and sat him down. He pulled out his handkerchief and handed it to Jo Jo. "Here, wipe your brow, but try not to puke in it. It's my Sunday handkerchief."

"Lord, Buck, I'm gonna die before I get to the river."

"No, you're not. You're gonna make it. If you die now, you'll go straight to Hell."

Jo Jo got his hands around Buck's waist and pulled himself to his feet. "What's my eyes look like now, Buck?"

"Aggies. Like all them marbles you won when you played us for keeps."

"I'll give 'em all back to you, Buck, I swear."

"Ain't no time to be worried about that now, Jo Jo. The river ain't far now."

By the time they had reached the river, Herschel was there with the preacher. Word had spread rapidly, and several members of the congregation were standing by the river bank. Sister Isabel Putnam, who played the organ, had pulled her skirt up and waded out into the river.

"Glory to God, this boy's coming to give himself to the Lord," yelled Buck to Brother Stegall.

Sister Putnam shook her skirt and yelled, "Hallelujah! Praise the Lord!"

Buck handed Jo Jo over to the preacher. By this time, Jo Jo was so sick he had gone into a state of semi-shock.

"I gotcha, son. Follow me out into the river. What a glorious day this is!" said Reverend Stegall.

Herschel came around to where Buck was standing. "We've done good, Buck. Brother Stegall's so happy he claimed we could take up the collection next Sunday."

Brother Stegall had waded with Jo Jo into the river. They stood about six feet from Sister Putnam, who was still shouting.

Brother Stegall placed one hand on Jo Jo's back and the other one on his head. "Brothers and sisters, we have found the lost sheep, and the Good Shepherd is about to welcome this here boy to His fold."

Jo Jo looked over at Reverend Stegall. "Hurry, Reverend Stegall, put me down in the water."

Reverend Stegall looked at the crowd that had gathered on the bank. "Listen to him. Listen to this here boy so anxious to be saved. Glory to God."

Reverend Stegall lowered Jo Jo into the river and said, "Do you take the Lord Jesus Christ to be your Savior?" and Jo Jo felt the water cover his head. The water brought Jo Jo back to his senses. He opened his eyes and came face to face with a large cottonmouth.

Jo Jo sprang up from the cool river, spitting water out of his mouth, and yelling, "Holy sh–!"

Brother Stegall, in excitement, dumped Jo Jo again, shouting, "He's got the Holy Spirit!"

Once again Jo Jo went under the water to come face to face with the cottonmouth. And once again he sprang up.

"Whatcha feel like, son?"

"Cotton..!"

Brother Stegall pushed him down again. "Cotton ain't good enough. You got to get white as snow."

Herschel looked over at Buck and said, "He's taking this more seriously than I thought he would, Buck."

Brother Stegall was quoting Scripture. Sister Putnam was singing "Amazing Grace."

By this time, the cottonmouth was tired of the invasion of his privacy and bit Jo Jo on the arm. Jo Jo came up screaming, "Je-sus Christ!"

The preacher pushed him under again. "That's right, Jo Jo, Jesus Christ, your accepted Savior!"

Along with the cottonmouth, Jo Jo's life began to unfold before his very eyes. It wasn't his big sins, but the little sins he saw, like shooting all Mr. Horn's chickens, hiding the school flagpole on the 3rd of July, putting his private in Mr. Pedigo's milking machine.

This time Jo Jo came up with the cottonmouth wrapped around his arm.

"Lord God, Buck, he's took up the serpent!"

"I don't think so, Herschel. Looks like he's trying to put it down."

Reverend Stegall cut his eyes toward Jo Jo's arm. "What you got there, boy?"

"It's a damn cottonmouth!"

Sister Putnam screamed, threw her skirt above her head, and started running to the bank. Reverend Stegall dropped Jo Jo and beat Sister Putnam to the bank.

Herschel and Buck were standing on the bank, yelling, "Get outta the water, Jo Jo! Get outta the water!"

Billy Thrasher was standing on the river bank. "Get him in the pickup. We gotta get him to the hospital."

By this time, Jo Jo's arm was beginning to swell bigger than his leg.

Billy Thrasher pulled out in his pickup with Jo Jo, Herschel and Buck in the back. Familiar houses and trees went by in a blur for Jo Jo. What was ninety miles an hour seemed to be a snail's pace for a dying boy. Jo Jo was shaking with chills and yelling, "I'm gonna die! I'm gonna die!"

"No you ain't, Jo Jo. No, you ain't. We're gettin' you to the hospital. Just hang on."

Jo Jo looked up at Buck and said, "You can't let me die, Buck. You can't let me die."

"We ain't gonna let you die, Jo Jo. You gotta be baptized again. That one didn't take."

The Dinner Bell

"Pardon me, sir, I don't mean to wake you."

The farmer pushed back his old sweaty straw hat which had been shading his closed eyes and rubbed his bushy gray eyebrows.

"That's okay. Weren't sleepin' anyway. I always come out here before lunch. Kinda rock and rest my eyes."

"You got a nice porch here."

"Yep, spend a lotta time out here. Figure I deserve it after spending all them years in the cornfields. Ain't seen you around these parts before," said the farmer.

"Well, I don't get to Bell Buckle very often," said the young man.

"Just as well. Ain't much happenin' here, anyway."

"I was told you own the farmhouse across the road."

"Ain't much of a farm. Just a few acres of land left and an old farmhouse 'bout to fall in. Don't tell me you're one of them city slickers looking for a place in the country?"

"No, I'm a city slicker looking for an old dinner bell. I noticed one in the back of the old house over there. Thought perhaps you'd sell it."

"It ain't in good condition...rusted out a lot. Don't know if it still has a clapper in it or not."

"Well, sir, it doesn't have to be in top-notch condition. That's what makes it old."

"Let me yell to the missus. She's about got lunch ready."

The old farmer opened the front screen door. "Mama, I'm taking someone across the road. Won't be gone long." He turned to the young man, "We can walk over. The weeds are kinda growed up. Ain't scared uh snakes, are you?"

The young man arched his eyebrows and said, "Wouldn't want to tangle with a rattler."

"They're out here in these parts. Charlie Lamb killed a six-

29

footer last week."

"I always heard they wouldn't hurt you if you don't bother them," said the young man.

"Well, I wouldn't want one to make you hurt yourself."

"Tell you what," replied the young man, "if one gets after us, you just spit that tobacco between his eyes. Your aim seems pretty good."

"Watch your step over here. Lots of old boards with rusty nails and broken glass around here. They'd go right through them new tennis shoes."

"If you don't mind my asking, what did you have to pay for a place like this?"

"Twelve thousand dollars. Bought it for the land. House ain't no good–gonna have her bulldozed down. Turn the land for pasture. Put some calves over here."

"Mind if I go in the house?"

"Reckon not, if we can get in. Be careful where you step–big holes in the floor. Wouldn't want you to get hurt. Look at all those beer cans. Sallie Tishner would turn over in her grave. Never allowed alcohol in here. Kids come here all hours of the night and party. Be glad when it's torn down. Get rid of this mess."

"It's a shame to see a house run down like this."

"It's been run down a long time. Old man Tishner died two years ago. His widow lived eighteen months after that. Watch that loose plank. Me and the missus tried to help the old woman best we could. Seems after Mr. Tishner died she didn't have much to live for. She and the old man are buried on the hill. I put a fence around the graves to keep the cows out. Watch for those broken windows. Darn kids come here, break out all the windows, play them radios loud!"

"Oh, they don't mean any harm," said the young man.

"Mean any harm? Just look at this place! Them walls there–can you believe what they've writ on them walls? Why, I wouldn't even let my missus come over here and see this."

"Well, I guess young people today are more liberal in their thinking."

"Yeah, well, when I was a young boy, liberal was politicians' talk. Boy, I didn't catch your name."

"Uh-h, Graffiti."

"Graffiti! What kinda name is that? Italian or somethin'?"

"Well, I don't know where it came from, but it's American now."

"Guess this place holds a lot of memories for someone."

"No, boy, houses don't hold memories; people hold memories. The old woman had a lot of memories–talked about her son a lot. She hadn't seen him in years. He lived in New York City–some kind of artist. Miss Sallie said someday he'd be well known. She showed me a picture he'd painted. It was supposed to have won an award, but if you ask me, he'd been better off if he'd come home and painted the house. I believe she called him Bill...naw, Will, that was it, Will."

"What happened to the painting?"

"Went to auction, furniture and all. The old man and woman run up a lot of medical bills. First him, then her, being so sick. That's how I come by the house, bought it at the auction. It weren't hardly worth the money, but what is these days?"

"How long have you been living across the road?"

"About five years. Had a big farm over in Manchester but gave it to my boy. Me and the missus decided it was too much for us. So we come over here and bought this small place–not as much to take care of. Watch that roof there; it's about to fall in. Don't really need this here place. Just bought it so I can keep them darn kids out and keep someone from building across from me. What you gonna do with the dinner bell?"

"It's on my list."

"You city folks get me. Always comin' through the country buying anything. Feller come through here last week–big lawyer from Nashville, looking for a horse collar. Wanted to make a mirror. I had one in the barn. Hadn't used it in ten years–just hadn't bothered to throw it away. Give me ten dollars. Can you beat that? I walked to Patience, my old mule, looked her straight in the eye and said, 'Patience, you stuck your head in that old collar for years–now that city slicker's gonna see his head in it.' Can you imagine that? Guess that's what a college education can do for you."

"I take it you're not much on higher education?"

"Don't mind education; it's what you do with it. Did you notice that log cabin on the right just before you got here? Well, a city slicker bought it last year–a retired banker. Twice a week I have to go down and pull his tractor out of the ditch. That's what I'm talking about. He oughter had sense enough to of stayed at the bank and not got out on no farm. See that old plow in the field? Belonged to old man Tishner. Hasn't been used in years, but one day some city dude will come by here, pay me good money to make a mailbox out of that old plow. People crazy–buy anything. Antique dealers come through all the time buying up old milk cans, old farm tools–paying good money for this old junk."

"It's a phase we're going through. It's called nostalgia," said the young man.

"It's called insane, if you ask me! A feller come through here the other day, offered me fifty dollars for an old bathtub on legs. I had it out in the field catching water for the calves. I figure if it's worth fifty dollars to him, it's worth fifty dollars to me. You'd never believe what the feller wanted to do with it. Said he wanted to take it home, paint it, put it on a platform in his bathroom, and put drapes around it. If you ask me, a feller has to be turned mighty peculiar to want to do that."

"Well, in the city we call it 'different strokes for different folks.'"

"What kinda talk is that? You sound like one of them kids that come here. That's the trouble with the world today, different strokes for different folks. That's the ruination of our country."

"Well, I didn't mean to upset you."

"You ain't upset me. You made me mad. Look at this house! Young people have no regard for anything. The Tishner boy never even come home for his father's or his mother's funeral. That's what I'm talkin' about. Just no respect for nothing."

"Just where is it written that a son must come home for his father's and mother's funerals?"

"Where is it written? Boy, it ain't never had to be written before. It's just respect! The boy never even come home to see about his mama. That old man and woman lived their lives for that boy. For years they sold off land, just so he could stay in New York. He never even checked on 'em."

"Well, maybe he just wasn't the kind that liked to write."

"Well, he didn't mind writin' home for money!"

"Now you said the boy was in New York, right?"

"Yep."

"Well, just suppose that when the father died, he didn't have the money to come home on."

"Well, he could of got here if he'd wanted to. That's no excuse. Besides, he was doing all right when his mama died. He'd won an award for that dang picture."

"Now, just suppose when his mother died, there was nothing left to come home for. Besides, winning an award doesn't mean money in your pocket. It just means somebody recognized your work."

"Recognized your work?" said the farmer. "I wish you could have seen that picture. It was called 'Sunrise.' But I don't know how you could of recognized it. Miss Sallie called it abstract. Sunrise, my behind! I ain't never seen no sunrise like that. It hung right over there. See on that old wall? You can still tell where it hung. Miss Sallie looked at it for hours. Sometimes that was the only sunshine the old lady had; Lord, the suffering Miss

Sallie went through!"

"She suffered?"

"Suffered! Lord, yes, but that wouldn't hold a candle to her broken heart. Just look at that hill, boy. They're gone–won't be back this way again."

The young man looked through a broken pane to the hillside. "Why did you let her suffer?"

"Why did we let her suffer? We didn't break her heart. But I'll tell you one thing; we buried her in style. Even on her deathbed she asked that what little money she had left be sent to her son. She didn't know that what little money she had left was spent a long time ago. But we buried her right. That hillside was covered with spring flowers. Her boy might not have been here, but everyone else was. That hillside–now there was a picture."

"That's a waste of money! Dead folks can't smell flowers."

"Well, it ain't all for the dead. It's for the living, but guess you wouldn't know much about that, boy."

"Well, at least she saw the Sunrise picture before she died," said the young man.

"Why the darn picture, you can't hardly hang it anywhere; it don't fit in the bedroom, and if you put it in the living room, people come in wondering what it is and thinking you're crazy. The bathroom is about the only place you can put it. At least your back is to it part of the time."

"Sounds to me like you bought the picture."

"What would I want with the picture? I told you I ain't seen no sunrise in it. What's that list you got that dinner bell on?"

"It's a game."

"What kinda game?"

"Oh, about five of us were going on vacation this year to different parts of the country. I had to come to Nashville on business, so I combined my vacation with the business trip."

"And that's a game?"

"Well, it's a game we're playing. A list was made of items to

34

bring back, and an old dinner bell was on it. Bet I'm the only one to find the bell."

"Well, this is it. Like I told you. It ain't much of a bell. Won't be no trouble gettin' it down, though. Post's already rotten."

"How much do you want for it?"

"Well, I don't know. How about twenty-five dollars?"

"That seems a little high."

"I figure anybody drivin' a big car like you can afford it. Besides, it's worth twenty-five dollars for me to come over here and walk through all this mess. Don't necessarily want to sell it. Had one man try to buy my barn–wanted to make it into a house. Can you believe that? Think we can get that bell in your trunk? If I sold the barn, wouldn't have no place to keep Patience. Feller said he'd make a place specially for Patience. Wouldn't want to do that to the mule. Patience wouldn't want to live with no kook."

"Well, I guess twenty-five isn't too much. Think you can help me carry it to the car?"

"Yeah, kinda heavy. Glad you just wanted the bell. Thought you might be one of the city slickers wantin' to buy the place. They worry me to death."

"Well, I didn't mean to disturb you. I just wanted the bell. I appreciate your helping me with it and all."

"I'll tell you what I'll do. We'll double or nothing," said the farmer. "If you can tell me what kind of tree that old stump was in the front yard, I'll give you the bell. If you miss, you owe me fifty dollars."

"How do I know you wouldn't trick me? I would say one thing, and you'd say something else."

"Boy, I ain't never tricked nobody in my life. Guess it, and the bell is yours."

"Well, from the looks of that old stump, I would say it's a maple."

"Well," said the farmer, "a maple it was, so it's your bell." He

35

shook his head. "I just don't understand why the Tishner boy wouldn't have painted that pretty old maple tree instead of some sunrise you can't make out."

"Sure you don't want the twenty-five dollars?"

"Naw, it's yours. How'd you get the trunk to pop open without a key?"

"A lever on the panel. Here, see?"

"Don't that beat all! What'll people think of next? Smell them beans and cornbread cooking? You're welcome to stay for lunch."

"Thank you, but I'm meeting a friend in Nashville for lunch."

"Lord, last time I ate in Nashville, I swore it was the last time. My fancy niece took me and the missus out to eat for our anniversary. Some place called the Hearth. Knew when I sat down to the table I was in trouble. Hadn't seen so much silver by my plate. Right then I knew it was going to be a lousy meal. First, they brought me some soup that didn't have nothin' in it. Then they brought out a snail and put it on my plate. Thought it must be a souvenir. Surely to God they didn't expect me to eat it. City folks don't know how to eat. They wouldn't know a biscuit from a door knob. You better eat here, or you're going to miss a good meal."

"Thanks again, but I've got to go. You take care of that picture you've got hanging in your bathroom. See you around."

The old farmer walked back up on his porch and into the kitchen.

"Daddy, that you? It's time for lunch. Who was that young man?"

"Said his name was somethin'–I can't remember."

"What'd he want?"

"His mama's dinner bell."

Prayer Meeting at the Christian Chapel

Preacher Haddock dreaded Wednesday night prayer meeting at the Christian Chapel. He knew that it ran a close second to the Friday night fights on TV. The only difference was that the Friday night fights were fake and the Wednesday night prayer meeting was for real.

His church had been split in every direction, and that's how his congregation sat–in every direction. The small community of Lumleyville, Tennessee, could only support one church; therefore, where you sat was indicative of what you believed. Sunday mornings were not as heated as Wednesday nights. People still sat in their particular section, but they let the preacher have the floor. It was a time for solemn reverence to the Lord. However, Wednesday night prayer meeting was open for discussion.

Through the years, Preacher Haddock saw his people put distance between the pews of neighbors and even family. Years ago the congregation had split over whether or not Jesus had been touched before He ascended into Heaven. This caused quite a stir one Wednesday night. One side argued that not a single person would have touched Jesus after He arose from the grave because He was pure and untouchable. The other side argued that Jesus was a loving man and would never ascend to Heaven without hugging His disciples bye. This group became known as the "Touchers" and sat on the right-hand side of the church. Each side pulled out Scripture, then they pulled out interpretation, then they pulled out the old Christian boxing gloves. Each went to his or her corner with Preacher Haddock trying to referee. Sister Lokey told that Thomas had stuck his finger in Jesus' side, and that was why he was called doubting Thomas, but some of the members paid no attention because they didn't think women had the right to have a say in the church. This group split off and sat in one of the Sunday School rooms. The church had several Sunday School rooms that opened up into the main congregation sitting room. That way everyone could still be a part of the service. The only difference was that the Sunday School classes did not have pews, but old fold-up, slatted chairs which squeaked a lot and caused distraction at the service.

However, this distraction was nothing compared to the day Dan Hackleberry spoke in tongues. This nearly caused several of the members to leave the church altogether and go over to one in the next community. Preacher Haddock convinced them, though, that the Holy Spirit worked in mysterious ways and all should be included in the house of the Lord. And so the first two pews on the left-hand side became known as the "Tongues." They were a small group that had received baptism by the Holy Spirit and spoke in a language that was provided by the Holy Ghost. Most of the rest of the left-hand side of the Christian Chapel was occupied by the "Sprinklers." Since the church had no baptistery, the congregation had to go to the nearby creek to be baptized. This caused quite a problem in the winter, so many of the brethren adopted the belief that a small amount of water could be administered in the church. Several of the members said that Jesus had been immersed in the River Jordan and that was the only way. Others contended that it wasn't the amount of water that saved you, but that going through the motions of baptism was just as good. The "Tongues" argued that baptism by fire from the Holy Spirit was the only way.

The "only way" was a big part of the arguments at the Christian Chapel. Some thought the only way to have communion was every Sunday while others believed once a month was enough. They even argued over how to serve communion. Some felt wine should be served in little individual glasses that sat in little round holes in the communion server; others thought the wine should be served in a communal chalice and passed from person to person. The communal chalice finally won out; however, there were those who refused to drink after another person. Some argued that in this day and time there was just too much disease going around; others argued that the alcohol in the wine would kill any germs. Then there was Sister Price, who reminded them it wasn't wine at all but Welch's grape juice. So some dipped their wafers into the large cup. Therefore, communion was divided between dippers and sippers; even they wouldn't sit together.

There was one man who had been raised Catholic, and he sat at the back left-hand side of the Sunday School room, not because he was Catholic, but because he was married to Sister Katherine Beasley, who was prone to have fits. Sister Beasley had fallen out of a tree when she was nine; and, as a result, these past forty-nine years she had been plagued with seizures. The Beasleys sat in the back room so that when a seizure came on, Mr. Beasley could get up and shut the door to the Sunday School room. This way the service could go on without anyone being disturbed.

Preacher Haddock reached the church about six forty-five on Wednesday nights. This gave him fifteen minutes to turn on the heat and warm the place up. Many nights he thought maybe he should save on fuel bills since prayer meeting became so heated in its own right. Tonight the subject was to be miracles. How could anyone fight over miracles? After all, they were recorded everywhere in the Bible, so surely there would be no disagreement on this.

As the seven o'clock hour approached, the pews filled with lay preachers eager to share the thoughts bursting in their temples. An opening prayer was led by Brother Jerigan, who was a "Sprinkler." After prayer, the congregation sang "When We All Get To Heaven."

Even the music had been a catastrophe in the church. There were those who dug up the Scripture which read, "Make melody in your heart," and so they argued that the piano was wrong. The others argued that there were musical instruments all throughout the Bible, and they wanted the piano in the service. This argument had been settled long ago by having one verse of a hymn sung with piano accompaniment and the next verse sung a cappella. Those who were always mad didn't sing at all.

Preacher Haddock opened his Bible. "Tonight we are discussing miracles of the Bible. I'm sure many of you will have thoughts to offer on this, for the Word is full of occasions where miracles were performed, and today miracles are still witnessed by God's people."

Preacher Haddock stepped down from the pulpit as he did every Wednesday night so he could be just another voice in the congregation. Everyone agreed that miracles were of the greatest importance to the Bible. Brother Taylor said that he thought the miracles of Moses certainly had a message for the people of his day. Sister Shaw commented that the Immaculate Conception was one of the greatest miracles that God had performed. The discussion was going quite well until Brother Porterfield brought up as fact that miracles had ended with the crucifixion of Christ, and there had been none since the death of Jesus. Preacher Haddock's Adam's apple fell to his butt. Everything had been going so smoothly, and now Brother Porterfield had brought in a new wrinkle to iron out in the clothing of the Gospel.

"What do you mean?" asked Sister Price. "Miracles happen every day. Why, they happen all over the world, and if you don't believe in miracles, Brother Porterfield, you're in bad shape."

Brother Owens spoke up. "I have to take the side of Sister Price, Brother Porterfield. People are cured every day by the laying on of hands."

"I appreciate your thoughts, Brother Owens," said Carl Porterfield, "maybe you should be sitting with the 'Touchers.'"

A few of the members chuckled at Porterfield's joke, but most were eager to argue. Preacher Haddock did his best to cast his bread upon the water, but the fish went after the bait that had been thrown into the sea of Scripture. Preacher Haddock rubbed his head, for he knew that anytime the sea of Scripture rushed to shore, it took back out the sands of love and compassion that were contained within the walls of the Christian Chapel. Everyone got in on this one since they all knew of a miracle. And soon the hornets' nest burst, and the people were buzzing with stingers of contradiction.

Sister Price was a big woman who wore large print dresses and sensible shoes. Her deep alto voice was missed on the verses without the piano. She rose to her feet. "Brother Porterfield," she said, "I'm sorry you do not believe in miracles, but I can't believe you live in this day and time without noticing these occasions all about you. Why just a few days ago I read in the paper that somewhere in Estill Springs, Tennessee, the face of Jesus appeared on a freezer on someone's front porch. I don't think this would have made the news in papers around the country if it were not true."

"I saw the same article, Sister Price," Brother Porterfield said, smiling and nodding, "but I also recall some people thought the face resembled Willie Nelson. Now you can't tell me the face on the freezer is a miracle when you're not sure whose it really is."

"Well, if the people say it's Jesus, then I believe it's Jesus. Besides, Carl Porterfield, you wouldn't know Jesus if you saw Him. After all, you were sprinkled, and that won't get you to Heaven in a minute's breath." Sister Price sat down, picked up a hymnal, and began to fan herself with the back cover.

Brother Nance rose to the occasion. "I didn't read the article about Jesus' face on the freezer, but I did see in a magazine where the Virgin Mary appeared to several children in Yugoslavia. People from everywhere are going to visit this spot. I might even go myself."

Brother Jakes had sat quietly long enough. "Brother Nance, I tend to agree with Carl Porterfield. This face on the freezer and the Virgin Mary appearing to children seem to be farces. It appears this article about the face on the freezer lost some of its credibility. I read where some of the people have noticed that the face appears when the neighbor in the next-door trailer turns on his porch light. Maybe the shadows on the dents on the freezer do make an outline that resembles some face; however, I do not believe that Jesus would pick a freezer on someone's front porch in some little town in Tennessee to make an appearance. It's just some hysterical people in Tennessee like those children in that foreign country. There are no miracles today, and if you're looking for a sea to part, then you'd better read Moses, 'cause that's the only place you're gonna find it."

Brother Nance raised his voice with authority. "Brother Jakes, you have all the right to agree with Carl Porterfield. After all, this is a free country. And that's why we're free; we believe in the Bible. But I cannot discredit what those children saw. 'Blessed are the little children who come unto me,' said Christ, and I believe they saw the Virgin Mary. Why, they even described what she was wearing. It was a golden shawl. I don't believe those children would lie about such a serious matter."

"Well, I believe you believe it, Brother Jakes, but it sounds like baloney to me. What they probably saw was that nutty Shirley MacLaine on one of her outings. After all, that's her style. I just can't believe the Virgin Mary is crazy enough to go to Yugoslavia."

"Carl Porterfield, I think you're getting a bit sacrilegious here," shouted Caroline Price. "Just who in the hell do you think you are, trying to think for Mary? After all, she's the mother of Christ, and if she wants to go to Yugoslavia, she sure as hell can!"

"Please," shouted Preacher Haddock, but it did no good. By this time the "Tongues" on the front two rows on the left-hand side had gone into the Holy Spirit of things and were jabbering like it was the day of Pentecost. The Sunday School room was in a panic because Sister Price had spoken out and had done so with such bluntness. Sister Katherine Beasley had gone into one of her seizures, but this time her husband did not shut the door, for there was no need to. The whole church was in a fit.

Someone was heard yelling, "It's those darn Catholics' fault! They see miracles all the time, and would someone shut the Holy Rollers up up front." Brother Porterfield was heard shouting to Sister Price that the only miracle that she had seen was her idiot son finishing high school. Brother Nance pushed Mrs. Nance under the pew, for now and then a hymnbook sailed through the air like a ball from a cannon.

Preacher Haddock was at his wit's end. No one could hear him over the bedlam. The only thing left to do was create a diversion, so he jumped to the center of the congregation and began to pull his clothes off. As he pulled off his tie, shirt and coat, he tossed them in the air. Then came the undershirt and pants. A hush came over the brothers and sisters. Finally, something had gotten their attention. Preacher Haddock stood quietly in his blue boxer shorts, then Brother Jerigan spoke. "Preacher, don't you think you're gonna get a mite bit chilly?"

Children were heard asking, "Mama, why does Preacher Haddock have his clothes off?" Mamas hushed their children and then turned their heads.

Preacher Haddock started in a low, serious voice. "Yes, I've got my clothes off, and I'll keep stripping until all of you have shed your self-righteous rags. You're not behaving like Christians; you're acting like you're in a back-alley bar fight. I won't stand for it in this church! I want each one of you to go home and pray. Right now it would take a miracle to save this church. I don't want to see any of you till tomorrow night at seven o'clock. You think about what you've done here tonight, and tomorrow night I hope you'll ask for forgiveness. Now let's depart while there's still a little dignity left in us."

Slowly, the congregation filed out of the front doors. There were some whispers among the sisters and brethren, but no one raised a voice. Preacher Haddock walked home that night; he needed the fresh, cold air to comfort him. That night he prayed harder than he had ever prayed before.

The next morning Preacher Haddock got up with a heavy burden. He looked back on all the misunderstandings of the past years, but this one had them all beat. This time they had gotten bitter with each other. Even moving to a different section would not dissolve this argument; besides, there were no sections left to move to. Preacher Haddock saw the worst: the only thing left was for the church to dissolve. He had seen many churches fall by the wayside, like the one where he used to preach in Bell Buckle, Tennessee. Over coffee and morning biscuits, he could envision his current church standing empty, with white paint disappearing to gray, and rotten boards succumbing to weather. He could see the huge front doors resting on rusty hinges, moving to the whims of wind. He could imagine broken-down pews covered with dust and insects, insects that left their initials on wood. He could see hymnals scattered here and there, mildewed from the rain that poured through the rotting roof. He could hear rolling beer cans on uneven floors that hosted parties in the night. He could see his carved oaken pulpit in someone's den. The imagined broken window panes matched the broken heart within him. He was their leader, and he had led them to this. He searched his mind for an answer. There was a sermon he had preached as a student that might suit this situation, but it was packed away in the attic in some old papers.

Slowly, he climbed the attic stairs, weighed down with a heavy heart. It had been years since he had been in the old, cluttered, dark room upstairs. He remembered the light switch was on the left-hand wall. He ran his palm across the rough old boards; the switch had to be close. From the corner of his eye he noticed a glowing and wondered what was in the attic. His hand reached the switch and turned on the light. The glowing stopped when the light came on. Puzzled, he immediately switched the light off. There it was again, something glowing near the far corner of the room. Once again he switched the light on, and again the glow disappeared with the light. There was only one thing left to do: he would turn off the light and slowly approach the glow in the dark.

At any other time Preacher Haddock might have been a little scared, but his mind was crowded with problems and did not have room for fright. He had to be careful; the attic was full of old family belongings scattered here and there. He was almost to the corner; just a few more steps and he would have the glowing whatever in his hands. Quickly, he grabbed the object. His steps quickened on his way back to the light. He wasn't taking any chances. The thing was heavy and, not knowing what it was, he didn't want to hold it long. When he reached the light and flipped it on, he began to smile. The smile turned to a laugh, then the laugh turned to tears. For a moment he returned to his childhood.

When his mother died, he brought home the things that she had collected through the years and put them away in the attic. Among her collection was a two-foot statue of Jesus Christ that glowed in the dark. Back in the forties, a radio station in Del Rio, Texas, had a religious program that sold chenille bedspreads with the Lord's Prayer in the middle, rose bushes from the Garden of Eden, and two-foot statues of Jesus Christ that glowed in the dark. If none of this suited you, then you could order a hundred baby chicks guaranteed to arrive with ninety-seven living or your money back. He remembered his mother listening to the old radio show and ordering the statue.

He was about to put it back when a thought entered his mind. Maybe he could use this statue in tonight's talk. No, he couldn't; that would be deceiving, even if it did work and bring the people back together. He thought, then pondered. If this statue were to be set off in the distance, just far enough away from the congregation to see the glow.... No, he couldn't resort to tricks; after all, he was a man of God. Sticks turning to snakes were in Moses' day. He prayed on it all the same.

Lord, maybe You've given me a sign. I need a sign. If You've

45

ever given me a sign, do it now. Mama, is that you giving me help? You usta help me out of situations all the time. He prayed and clutched the statue. "I'll do it, Lord, whether it's You or Mama, since it just might be the thing I need to hold the church together."

He turned quickly and took the statue to the car, carefully placing it in the trunk, then driving to the church. He walked several hundred feet from the building and placed the statue in a clump of brush that could be seen from windows on the left-hand side of the chapel.

He remembered painfully how even the side of the church had been a thorn in his side. Some of the brethren noticed that the people who sat on the right-hand side were on the "right" side. Preacher Haddock settled this by saying that when you arrive, you come in on the right side, but when you leave, the left side becomes the right side. This, for the most part, kept them happy.

He returned home to wait for that evening's meeting.

People made a quiet entrance to the church that night. No one was speaking, with the exception of a few of the children, snickering and wondering if Preacher Haddock was going to take his clothes off again. Some parents even left the children at home since they didn't know what to expect that night.

Preacher Haddock opened the service by saying a prayer himself; he wasn't taking any chances. Afterwards they sang "Love Lifted Me," but it was very weak. Preacher Haddock went immediately into his message. "Brothers and sisters, I hope you've had time to think about what went on here last night. I know you're a kind and decent people who stick together like family. I've seen you come to each other's rescue in times of need on the farms and with friends. It is only in this churchhouse that you cannot get along. Of all places, in this churchhouse, a place where love is everything. Whether you believe in the miracles of yesterday or today is beside the point.

"Sister Price, I can remember the time you sat all night with

Brother Porterfield's wife and wiped her brow till the fever broke the next morning. Brother Nance, I can remember the day you helped pull Brother Jerigan's cow from the frozen creek. And when someone was without, you all have come to the rescue. There are so many things that you have done for each other in this small, wonderful community. Now let us join together and, Brother Porterfield, would you mind pulling the shade down, the one near your seat. There's something outside distracting me."

Brother Porterfield reached up to close the shade when he noticed a glow a few hundred feet away. "There's something out there. I can't make it out, but there's something glowing out there all right."

At that moment, the sisters and brethren started straining their necks to peer out the windows. "What is it?" was heard from several people. Some speculated that the moon was probably reflecting on a piece of tin.

Sister Price exclaimed, "It looks like Jesus!"

"Now there you go, Sister Price," snapped Carl Porterfield, "seeing things that ain't there."

Brother Nance shaded his eyes. "It does look like a man standing off in the distance."

"It's nothing but a piece of tin," said Porterfield.

"Well, why don't we go and see?" said Brother Jakes, starting to get up from his pew.

"No, honey, it might be a mad animal or something," Mrs. Jakes said as she pulled him back into his seat.

Then Brother Rutledge, usually a quiet man, started yelling. Since he seldom had anything to say in church, his yelling caused quite a stir. "Praise the Lord, I can see out of my left eye!" shouted Brother Rutledge.

"What do you mean you can see out of your left eye?" asked Sister Price. "You've been blind in it ever since that combine accident."

"I know, but when I looked at the glowing in the churchyard, my sight came back. I can see just like I did years ago! Praise the Lord!"

Sister Price shouted, "It's a miracle!" and soon the church was overjoyed.

Brother Porterfield asked, "How many fingers am I holding up, John Rutledge?"

John Rutledge answered, "Hold them all up, Carl Porterfield, I want to see them all!"

Even the skeptics were amazed. The image of the Lord had shone His light upon the Christian Chapel. Some started to argue that the glow looked more like the Burning Bush, but before things got out of hand, Preacher Haddock said, "Let us rejoice for Brother Rutledge. He was blind and now he sees. Let us pray for this moment. Now go your ways, and remember that this churchhouse was built out of love and not out of discontent."

The people rushed to John Rutledge and hugged him, then went to their cars to return home and talk about what they had just witnessed. Preacher Haddock stayed behind to turn off the stove and give thanks to the Lord and his mama. As he walked toward the front door, he noticed John Rutledge standing on the front steps. Preacher Haddock walked up and put his arm around the brother.

"Can you really see out of that blind eye, Brother Rutledge?"

Brother Rutledge smiled and with a twinkle in his good eye said, "Brother Haddock, years ago I usta listen to a radio station down there in Del Rio, Texas."

Preacher Haddock smiled. "Do you want to go with me to get it?"

"Why not, Preacher? I always wanted one."

The Leaf Falls Not Far From the Tree

Miss Sadie Tulu got up from her Queen Anne chair, walked across her Tabriz oriental rug, sat down to Limoges tableware, picked up her sterling Tiffany soup spoon, and stirred her coffee.

"Taffy Tulu, your dress is cut much too low to wear to the courthouse."

"But, Mother!"

"Too low, Taffy. No, I didn't mind when you bobbed your hair, and I held my tongue when the hemline moved up, but I will not have my daughter running around with her bosom showing."

Taffy looked down at her cleavage and wondered why mothers had to be so prudish.

"Hurry now, Taffy. Either change or go out to the summerhouse and gather some lilacs to pin to the front of your dress. Hurry, we mustn't be late."

"Mother, we shouldn't even be going to the courthouse. I don't want this divorce."

"Taffy Tulu, I know what's best for you, and this divorce is best for you."

"Mother, I love Clayton Crabtree and he loves me."

"Child, a marriage is more than love; besides, what do you know of love? You slipped off in the night with that Clayton Crabtree just like common white trash. Your grandfather built you this house, and I bought you everything to be well-bred, and you didn't even have a proper wedding. Your grandfather would turn over in his grave."

Miss Sadie stared at the mahogany staircase. "Oh, Taffy, I dreamed of you walking down those stairs in your beautiful white lace gown–slowly down the staircase, Taffy, and into the parlor where all the guests could see you and gasp at the beautiful young woman who was about to be wed to the handsome, well-bred young man. I can't believe you did this to me. I wanted it all to be so proper."

"Why has everything got to be so proper, Mother? I went to Memphis to Miss Hutchinson's Finishing School for Girls. I learned to walk with a book on my head, sit with my legs crossed just right, and learned how to crook my little finger when holding my demitasse cup. But that doesn't change anything, Mother; I still love Clayton. That's what's important."

"Taffy, come with me."

Miss Sadie grabbed Taffy by the arm and pulled her out onto the side porch. She took a deep breath and looked out over her vast grounds. "That's important, Taffy."

Miss Sadie pointed in all directions. "Land, girl, land. It's the most important thing in the world; next is bloodline."

Miss Sadie looked out at her cotton fields. On the distant horizon it looked as if the cotton touched the clouds.

"Do you see what I see? All that will be yours someday. I've worked myself to death making sure you had a future, a future with someone the town looks up to. Not trash like that no-good Clayton Crabtree. He just wants our land, Taffy; the object is to acquire land, Taffy, not give it away."

"Mother, we've got more land than anyone in Bedford County. We don't need any more."

"Child, you never have enough land. It's the land that bears the crops. It's land that's under houses, buildings, real estate, Taffy."

"Look at the real estate we have now, Mother. When poor people can't pay their rent, you make them move; townspeople are down on us, Mother. They say it isn't Christian of you."

"Lord, Taffy, will you ever learn? Who do you think I learned business from? The Lord, Taffy. The Lord Himself. He's the best businessman I know. He expects ten percent from everybody, and look what He's done with the money. Churches left the wildwood long ago. Now they're cropping up everywhere–Baptist, Presbyterian, Methodist, and look at the Catholics. He sure made a good investment there. The world moves on. A big hand just doesn't come out of space and stop the world from turning. Time doesn't stand still so people can wait to pay their rent. No, Taffy, the world keeps turning, and it is an idiot who tries to catch the wind and a fool who tries to stop time. Time doesn't stop for anybody. And that's what I'm trying to tell you, Taffy; in time, this will all be yours–this land, this house, all the furnishings I've hand-picked so you can have a good life. That's why you must leave Clayton Crabtree. You must marry a man with good breeding."

"*Nouveau riche*, Mother, that's French for 'new rich.' That's what they called us at Miss Hutchinson's Finishing School. They laughed at me, Mother. The girls laughed at me 'cause they knew we weren't old money. Theirs was handed down from generation to generation. Their grandfathers were colonels in the war. My granddaddy rode over these mountains with a carpetbag and took advantage."

"Taffy, this is 1925, not 1864! Your grandfather built this house 'cause he wanted us to have what he had never had growing up. He's the one who named you after the candy 'cause he knew how sweet you'd grow up to be. Why, he'd turn over in his grave if he could hear you speak of him like this."

"I don't mean to speak ill of grandfather, Mother; it's just we don't need to be something we aren't."

"We aren't going to be late to that courthouse. Pin some lilacs to your dress, and then we will speak no more of this nonsense. Go to the car."

"I've torn my silk hose; I've got to change them."

"Get in the car; we will not be late."

"We've got thirty minutes."

"We still need to hurry. We have much to do. I must stop by the poorhouse. I need workers for the land this afternoon."

"That's another thing, Mother. Townspeople are talking about the way you go down to the poorhouse and order those people to work for you. You don't even pay them!"

"They don't need paying. They're in the poorhouse now

51

'cause they can't manage money." Miss Sadie tugged at Taffy's arm, almost pulling her into the long black roadster. For several miles, Sadie would glance to the left, then to the right, admiring the rolling pastureland she loved so much.

Taffy shut her eyes to the vast land. Instead, she bounced memories off her closed eyelids. She remembered waltzing under sparkling stars on summer nights, walking barefoot hand-in-hand through sun-reflected creeks, chasing fireflies through the flowered meadows. Clayton had brought sequins to her swiss polka-dotted world.

"See out that window, child; we've been riding all this time, and we're still looking out at our own land. When we get this divorce, you'll marry good blood, Taffy, and then your son and your son's son will have this land."

"No good blood will want me, Mother. I'll be a divorcee. No decent man would want a second-hand woman for his wife. I'll be by myself for the rest of my life!"

"Nonsense, Taffy Tulu. Look at you! Why, you're prettier than any girl around; no one has your blonde hair, blue eyes, and cream complexion. You can have anyone you want."

"I want Clayton Crabtree. The man I married! Every girl in this county wanted him, but I got him! Now you're taking him away!"

"Taffy, you know that quarter horse in the stable–the one that can outdo any quarter horse in this county? He's a fine horse, Taffy, but you don't see anyone bringing their Tennessee Walker over here for stud service."

"Mother, we're talking about people, not horses!"

"We're talking about principle, Taffy."

"Principle!" shouted Taffy. "Mother, you compare everything to horses, land, poorhouses, and even God. Everything you think of goes back to money. Money can't buy happiness. And it can't buy Clayton Crabtree. He loves me, not your money."

"Taffy Tulu, how dare you talk to your mother like this. Why, your grandfather would turn over in his grave. Clayton Crabtree was after my money. He's the type, Taffy. I could buy and sell him every day of the week."

"He can't be bought, Mother. He loves me. Why, never once did he mention anything about money to me."

"You don't think he would, do you? A wolf never tells his intent in the henhouse."

"Oh, Mother, I can't talk to you. Everything is compared to something that has nothing to do with anything. Clayton can't be bought."

Taffy and Miss Sadie did not speak for a few minutes, then the silence in the roadster was broken.

"Clayton said you poisoned him, Mother."

"What did you say, child?"

"Clayton said you tried to poison him. He went to the doctor. The doctor confirms it. Oh, Mother, could you really do that?"

"No. If Clayton Crabtree got poisoned, he did it himself."

Miss Sadie's roadster came to a parking place outside the courthouse. Hurriedly, she got out and started up the steps.

"You speak nice to Judge Benson, Taffy. He'll be presiding over this meeting, and you let me do the talking."

The courthouse in Shelbyville, Tennessee, smelled like the train depot in Nashville, but Miss Sadie didn't pay any attention to the freshly disinfected, mopped, marble floors. It was the fragrance of lilacs on Taffy that she smelled. As she passed the polished brass spittoon, she glanced to see if her hat sat just right.

"Miss Sadie."

Judge Benson rose from his chair. His pin-striped arms reached for her. "I believe you know Mr. Jacobs, the attorney for Mr. Crabtree."

Miss Sadie nodded but did not speak.

"And Taffy, as always, you look delightful," said Judge Benson.

Taffy smiled and quickly glanced over to the man she had

married. His white linen suit against his tanned skin and dark hair made him even more handsome. He did not stand but sat with his flat straw hat in his hands. He tried not to look at Taffy but stared off at the unfinished George Washington portrait.

"Now, Miss Sadie, we will get down to business. I have before me papers that will dissolve this marriage between Taffy Tulu and Clayton Crabtree. Now, are there questions or statements either party would like to make at this time?"

Jack Jacobs cleared his throat and stood up.

"Judge Benson, I have here before me certified papers from a doctor that Miss Sadie tried to poison her son-in-law."

Miss Sadie slowly turned her head toward the attorney and said, "Mr. Jacobs, we are here for a divorce–not because Mr. Crabtree has been ill."

"Quite ill, Miss Sadie," snapped the attorney.

"I'm sorry that Mr. Crabtree has not felt well, Mr. Jacobs, and, Your Honor, I will not listen to this foolishness of poisoning."

"Miss Sadie, Mr. Jacobs, this is a serious accusation," said Judge Benson.

"Quite serious, Your Honor," replied the attorney.

Clayton sat quietly, still holding his hat. He glanced quickly at Taffy, who immediately turned away in embarrassment.

"Here are the records, Your Honor, that document my client's visits to his doctor and indicate that he was near death."

"Near death!" screamed Miss Sadie. "Clayton Crabtree, the closest you've been to Huggins Funeral Home is that picture on the fan that Mr. Jacobs is fanning like a monkey with. My money, that's what you're after!"

"Your Honor, if I might proceed, these medical reports prove that the poison was ingested by Mr. Crabtree in small degrees. The doctor states it was most probably administered in his tea."

"Mr. Jacobs, this is a most serious accusation."

"I have the papers to prove the allegations, Your Honor."

"Mr. Jacobs, you have proof of poisoning on paper, but you do not have proof that it was done by Miss Sadie."

"Your Honor, the doctor has recorded that the poisoning was most probably administered in the tea. Miss Sadie insisted Mr. Crabtree join her for tea and honey biscuits every afternoon. And Miss Sadie has the motive to get rid of her son-in-law as shown in this court today."

"Judge Benson, if Mr. Crabtree accidentally stirred his tea with rat poisoning instead of sugar, it is not my fault, and I dare not be held responsible."

"Mr. Benson, unless you have positive proof of Miss Sadie's intent, this charge will have to be dismissed."

"Your Honor, I feel my client's illness, doctor bills, and other inconveniences are worthy of compensation."

"Judge, we are here to dissolve a marriage, not compensate any stomachache Mr. Crabtree may have encountered. Money! See, I told you, Judge Benson, it's my money he's after!"

"Miss Sadie, I doubt Mr. Crabtree is after your money. After all, he has a substantial amount of his own."

"Never enough, Judge. No one ever has enough!"

"Now, if we can continue on the issue of why we're meeting here," said the judge, looking over his glasses. "Petition has been filed by Miss Taffy Tulu to have her marriage to Mr. Clayton Crabtree dissolved. Is there any statement from either of you?"

Taffy leaned forward as if to speak but leaned back in her chair at the cut of Miss Sadie's eyes.

"Your Honor, I'd like to say that I love Taffy, and I know it is her mother who is responsible for this divorce."

"Mr. Crabtree, how much were your medical bills?" asked Miss Sadie.

"Several thousand dollars!" answered the lawyer quickly.

"Then do you think ten thousand would settle your stomach, Mr. Crabtree?"

"I think that would be sufficient," replied the lawyer.

Clayton glanced at Taffy for one last reaction. Taffy shut her eyes.

"Yes, ten thousand, ten thousand should suffice," said Clayton.

"Then, Mr. Jacobs, show it in the papers that this marriage is dissolved and let there be a statement showing a settlement of ten thousand dollars."

"Thank you, sir," replied the lawyer.

Miss Sadie quietly rose and took Taffy by the arm. "And I trust, Mr. Crabtree, that you will not be interfering with my household again."

Miss Sadie hurriedly escorted Taffy from the room to avoid further conversation. As they walked down the corridor together, Taffy wanted to cry but held back the tears. Miss Sadie arched one eyebrow and glanced at Taffy with that "I-told-you-so" look. Finally, Miss Sadie sighed and said, "If your grandfather knew what we'd been through today, Taffy, why he'd turn over in his grave."

"I sure hope he's comfortable in his resting place, Mother, since he has to turn over so much."

"Taffy Tulu, what am I going to do with you? You have no respect for the living or the dead."

Just at that moment, Taffy noticed a young man coming toward them in the corridor. "There's Henry Moss, Mother. He's originally from Bell Buckle, but now he's a reporter for the *Nashville Banner*. Hi, Henry," Taffy said, half smiling.

"Hi, Taffy."

Miss Sadie glanced at the young man; his straw hat pushed back on his head made his curly hair fall across his forehead.

"Henry, this is my mother, Miss Sadie. Mother, this is Henry Moss. I met him at a dance in Nashville. Henry, what are you doing in Shelbyville?"

"I'm here to cover a lawsuit over a government dispute. Perhaps I may call on you, Miss Taffy."

"That would be nice, wouldn't it, Mother?"

"Why, yes, Taffy, that would be nice. Perhaps you might like to ask Mr. Moss over for tea and biscuits sometime."

The Confederate

Jack Ledbetter didn't make any will; he knew he'd be coming home. That's the way southern men thought when they went off to fight the Great War. Lincoln was in the White House, but the South's allegiance was turned to Montgomery, Alabama, and it was a different flag that prompted hands to salute and to cover the heart. Jack knew his time had come. He had to take part in history. No longer could he be a bystander; his duty was to the Gray.

Jack laid the muzzle-loader across his lap, and with a soft cloth he began to polish the walnut stock until his face reflected on the grain. He oiled the hammer and trigger. A man's life depended on his gun–it had to be in perfect order and shape. Jack had come by a Springfield, the prize gun to hold. He carefully aimed the long barrel into the air and made sure the sight was accurate. A fraction off could mean life or death.

The gray uniform Jack was so proud of was carefully placed over the back of a chair. The buttons and braid were shining like California gold.

Jack Ledbetter, Jr. stood at the doorway watching his daddy preparing for battle. Junior, known as Son Jack, entered the room.

"Can I go with you, Daddy?"

"No, son, this is a man's war. It's no place for an eight-year-old. Someday you'll be old enough, but not today."

"You gonna whip them Yankees, ain't ya?"

"I'm gonna shoot those blue devils right between the eyes and watch 'em squirm."

Son Jack watched his father place the gun carefully by his uniform.

"Someday this will be your gun, son. You must always take care of it. A good soldier never is away from his gun. You never know when you might need it. Many a soldier died 'cause some

59

Yankee slipped up on him and his gun wasn't handy."

A few minutes later, Jack and Son Jack were interrupted by Cathy Ledbetter, who burst into the room and turned the TV knob–as she did every day at three o'clock to hear: "As sands through an hourglass, so are the days of our lives."

"Jack, what have I told you about a gun in the house? Put that thing in the attic or in the dump–I don't care which one, just get it out of here. And while you're at it, take that silly uniform and give it to the Salvation Army. No, better yet, throw it in the dump, too."

"It's not a silly uniform, Cathy. That's a Confederate uniform, and I'm wearing it tomorrow in the battle. I'm proud of it."

"Proud of it! Every five years a bunch of grown men dress like toy soldiers and fight a war that took place over a hundred years ago. It shouldn't have been fought then, and it damn sure doesn't need to be fought now."

"Then just tell me how you're gonna preserve our heritage? How are our sons and daughters gonna know what it was like to stand for pride and honor for a way of life?"

"What way of life? Overseers of a bunch of cotton balls? Too bad you couldn't shoot with them; maybe you'd have won the war."

"What makes you so damn sure we didn't win the war?"

"Well, I could have sworn Lee rode to Appomattox to meet Grant for something. Maybe it was for tea. Two opposing generals do that quite often. All I know is when Lee left, the North seemed to be mighty happy."

"Well, if..."

"Hush, I can't hear the TV. They're trying to catch the riverfront slasher. Oh God, Kimberly's about to be stabbed!"

"You object to me taking part in a battle in history, and you subject yourself to that garbage on TV. At least I'm with my buddies and not with a bunch of prostitutes and riverfront rippers."

"Will you shut up! I've been watching this show for years.

And Kimberly is not a prostitute. She's undercover for the cops. She hasn't been a prostitute for two years."

"Why do you watch this trash?"

"It takes my mind off cooking meals, washing dishes, cleaning house, going to the grocery store, running all the errands, and picking up your socks. And there's more–I'm just too tired to rack my brain.

Son Jack, don't you have anything to do?"

"No, ma'am."

"Maybe he can watch this crap with you." Jack turned his son toward the TV.

"See, son, this is what your mother thinks life's all about. Maybe she'd like for you to grow up to be perverted like some of them."

Cathy turned Son Jack away from the TV. "I've never let him watch the soaps. I have better sense. However, you'd have him raised to get all liquored up with his buddies and fight each other like some silly-ass schoolboys. Let it die. It's over. Done with. Forget it!"

"Forget it! My great-granddaddy died in that war. I suppose you'd like me to forget him, too."

"I can't help it 'cause your great-granddaddy lost his head. It doesn't mean you've got to lose yours."

"Well, your great-granddaddy sure didn't lose his. He sat on a porch in Kentucky and watched the rest of the world go by."

"You should set that to music. You could sing it tomorrow, right after everyone stands for 'Dixie.'"

"And what's wrong with 'Dixie,' may I ask?"

"Nothing, if you sing it in the shower!"

"I'll sing it where and when I want to, and I want to sing it tomorrow while I'm standing with the Gray. And if you don't like it, you don't have to be there."

"Don't worry, I wouldn't be caught dead there, but you probably will. Have you drawn straws to see who dies and who lives?"

"For your information, I'm one of the ones who lives."

"Well, Lord, if they just could have done that in the real war, it would have taken out all of the suspense. Maybe your great-granddaddy would have drawn the right straw instead of being buried somewhere in Ohio, and God knows where that is; you haven't found the grave yet."

"Well, I just..."

"Oh, my God, she's not going to have his baby, is she?"

Jack Ledbetter stormed out of the house and Son Jack went out to play.

Later that afternoon Son Jack saw Mrs. Winnett, a widow who depended on him to mow her lawn and do small errands, pull into her driveway. She was returning with grocery bags in her arms, and Son Jack always knew he could depend on a twenty-five cent tip for helping with the sacks. Although Mrs. Winnett lived alone, she always had at least six to eight sacks of groceries because she loved baking pies, cakes, and biscuits to share with the neighbors.

"Thank you, Son Jack. I bet you'd like a piece of pecan pie just now; we'll have ice cream on top. Just set those sacks where you usually do. Want chocolate or vanilla?"

"Chocolate."

"So, what have you been into today?"

"Oh, just knocking around and watching daddy get ready for war."

"What war?"

"The one great-granddaddy lost his head in."

"My word!"

"I don't reckon they ever found it. Guess it rolled down the hill like a hard biscuit. Might even rolled between some Yankee's legs. Who knows; it might still be rolling."

"My word!"

"'Course, then, someone might have found it, but they wouldn't know what body to put it with. It's lost, too."

"My word!"

"Then I guess it don't matter. The worms would have eaten it a long time ago. I don't reckon they embalmed then. They just buried you where you fell. No doctor or nothing to really know you're dead. Wonder how many they buried alive?"

"My, do you mind handing me that wet dish towel? I think I need it on my face."

"I wonder how long it takes worms to eat a body. I reckon by now great-granddaddy's picked clean."

"Son Jack, do you mind putting the milk in the refrigerator? I need to lie down a minute."

"Sure, Mrs. Winnett. Are you sure you don't want to finish your pie?"

"No, thank you. Just make sure the milk's put up. I'll do the rest in a little while."

"Yes, ma'am."

Later, when supper was served at the Ledbetter home, no one spoke. Through the evening, the silence became louder and louder. Cathy did the dishes, Jack tinkered in the garage, and Son Jack read his comic books. Son Jack noticed that the couch in the living room had been made for his daddy. He figured that must be some kind of custom for a man going off to war.

The next morning was Saturday, and Jack rose to the occasion. Cathy had left the house early to visit a friend in Bell Buckle. If Jack were persistent in this playing war, at least she wouldn't have to see him in his uniform carrying a gun.

That morning an excitement roared through the town of Rejoice, Tennessee. Liquor stores were busier than usual. Blue and Gray uniforms were seen in every direction. Confederate flags draped the courthouse square, and bugles were blowing in the wind. It was a time for rejoicing in Rejoice.

About two miles outside of town a battleground was marked where the skirmish was to take place. It was on the exact spot where the conflict was fought years before. Bleachers were set up to hold the crowd. A special platform had been erected for public officials. The battle was to begin at ten a.m., and by nine-thirty the bleachers were full. People had brought picnic lunches, and the local Lions Club was selling barbecue. Son Jack had arrived with his daddy but soon hooked up with his classmate, Tommy Lee. The boys sat on the ground near the official platform.

The long anticipated hour at last approached, and the Honorable Mayor Beachboard got up to introduce the Reverend Jacobs for the opening prayer. The Reverend prayed for God to bless the country and community. He continued to bless all the sick and shut-ins and others who could not attend this special event. He prayed for rain to come and bless the farmers everywhere. After what seemed an eternity, the Reverend Jacobs sat down and Mayor Beachboard got up to call on the sheriff to lead in the Pledge of Allegiance to both flags present. After the Pledge of Allegiance, Sister Doris Bell led the crowd in a rousing rendition of "Dixie," while everyone stood and sang, their hearts bursting with pride.

The actual battle had only lasted one hour and twenty-six minutes; however, Rejoice had turned it into a two-day event. Finally, Mayor Beachboard assisted Estelle Parkinson, local president of the United Daughters of the Confederacy, to the mike, then returned to his seat. Miss Estelle, a small woman in her eighties, had weakened through the years, yet she retained a strong memory.

"My friends, it is an honor for me to stand before this crowd. We of the United Daughters of the Confederacy have pledged to remember our men in Gray. We must remember that this red corsage I wear upon my bosom stands for the blood that ran across the Southland over one hundred years ago. We must remember our place in history in this nation. We must keep alive the memory, for it is the memory that keeps us alive."

Miss Estelle went on to give the history of the community. Right before she sat down, she raised a white-gloved fist into the air as she proclaimed, "We must stand fast!" With that, the charge bugle sounded and the battle began.

Son Jack watched his daddy run into battle. Cannons were going off and horses were rearing up. The crowd was cheering the Gray and booing the Blue. Swords were waving like windmills; rifles and pistols sounded like the Fourth of July.

"Boy, they really get into this, don't they, Tommy Lee?"

"Yeah, my old man got his leg broken five years ago. He fell off a horse, so this year he's standing on the ground."

Everyone watched for hours as the Blue and the Gray advanced and retreated. Those men who had drawn the straw to die somehow got up from the dead and kept the battle going. Blood was everywhere as men were moaning and crawling on the ground. The fake blood was apparently not needed. Mayor Beachboard, who was known to take a drink, was overheard saying, "This is the damnedest thing. Fake blood, just like in the movies."

Miss Estelle pulled out her lace handkerchief and waved the Gray on. "Give 'em hell, boys!"

"Why, Miss Estelle, I never heard you cuss before," remarked Reverend Jacobs.

Miss Estelle turned to the Reverend and quoted her favorite line from *Gone With the Wind*. "Reverend Jacobs, this is a war, not a tea party!"

Reverend Jacobs, who had moved into town only a few years before, leaned over and asked Miss Estelle, "By the way, who won this battle?"

"It ain't important who won it then; it's who's winning it now, Reverend. But for your information, they won it years ago!"

The Reverend was never sure who "they" were. He only knew Miss Estelle was in her glory.

By that afternoon stretchers were carrying off the real wounded and those playing dead. It was always a chore getting men to play the Blue. So it was devised that if you were Gray one year, you had to be Blue the next time.

Tommy Lee yanked Son Jack by the shirt. "Ain't that your daddy lying there with a bayonet in his butt?"

"Lord, my mama's gonna really be mad now. You reckon he's just pretending?"

"If he is, he's pretending mighty real. I think he's yelling for help."

"I need to help daddy."

"Are you crazy? You want to be trampled by a horse?"

"I can't let him die out there!"

"What straw did he draw?"

"To live."

"Well, I think someone got mixed up."

Son Jack ran to the men responsible for the stretchers. "Quick, my daddy's been hurt. Real hurt, not pretend hurt!"

"Which one is he, son?"

"Over there. See the one with the bayonet in his butt?"

The two men rushed in with the stretcher. They weren't sure if they should remove the bayonet or wait and let the doctor do it.

"Let's get him to the ambulance; they'll know what to do."

"If we can find one! They seem to be coming and going a lot."

"Look, there's one over there. He's coming toward us. Hey, over here! We got a wounded one!"

By now Jack had passed out from loss of blood. The ambulance attendant grabbed a blanket. "We've got to cover him up, keep him from going into shock."

Son Jack was right beside the stretcher as they loaded his daddy into the ambulance. The medics had managed to bring Jack around by the time they had reached the hospital.

"I gotta call mama and tell her you've been hurt."

"No, son, don't worry your mama; I'll be all right."

"But, Daddy, you've lost a lot of blood, and they say it's a nasty cut. Mama needs to be here."

"Don't call your mama!" Jack insisted as they rolled him into the emergency room, where Blue and Gray were everywhere. Dr. Gott was overheard saying, "My God, the whole Civil War wasn't this bloody!"

Pin-striped ladies had been called in to help with the insurance papers. Cannon Foster, who fought for the Blue, was yelling, "Jesus Christ, I got a mini-ball in my gut and you're wanting to know what my mother's damn maiden name was!"

"Now, Cannon, that's no way for a southern gentleman to talk," Martha Jordan cajoled.

"Hell, I'm no southern gentleman today. I'm a son-of-a-bitching Yankee!"

"Well, in that case, Cannon Foster, we just may let you die."

Son Jack waited in the emergency room lobby while his father was attended to. He knew he really needed to call his mama, but his dad had insisted. About thirty minutes later, the doctor came out.

"Son Jack, your father's going to be fine. He's lost a lot of blood, so we're keeping him overnight for blood transfusions and observation. He's got thirty-two stitches and he's weak, but he'll be OK. You can go with him to his room."

A few minutes later Jack was rolled down a corridor to his room. Son Jack sat by the bedside and watched his daddy slip in and out of sleep. About an hour later, Jack turned to his son.

"You didn't call your mama, did you?"

"No sir, but she's gonna wonder where you are. We got to tell her something; she's bound to notice a rip in your behind!"

Jack, Sr. and Son Jack didn't have long to ponder the story they needed to make up. Someone had already called Cathy, and she was on her way to the hospital. Her emotions were mixed. "Damn him, he deserves whatever happened, but, God, let him be all right!" As she approached Jack's room, Son Jack jumped up.

"Here's mama, Daddy. I didn't call her, I swear!"

"Well, you should have. I had to hear it from my next-door neighbor. Are you all right?"

"Yes, just some loss of blood and got a few stitches."

"Thirty-two stitches, Mama, but the doctor says he'll be fine."

"What happened?"

"I got stuck with a bayonet."

"Good Lord, Jack! You could have died, and I don't look good in black!"

"Well, I didn't."

It's by the grace of God that you didn't. Have you seen the emergency room lately?"

"OK, OK, you're right. I could have really been hurt. It was a foolish thing I did."

"Well, I'm glad you admitted to that. Where's your cut?"

Jack almost whispered, "In the butt."

"Where? You're mumbling so."

"In the butt, Mama."

Cathy Ledbetter thought for a moment, then she began to snicker. As her snicker turned into laughter, the laughter turned into bent-double, side-holding hysterics.

"I don't see what's so damn funny."

Cathy ran into the bathroom.

"See that. I'm lying here with thirty-two stitches, and your mother's in the bathroom wetting her pants."

Jack raised himself up from the bed.

"Is it funny enough? Can you hear me in there? That's OK, honey, I'll be all right. I could have bled to death, but I didn't. Listen to her. Do you think you can compose yourself by tomorrow? That's when I get to go home."

Jack looked over at his son with complete disgust as Cathy returned to Jack's bedside. Jack stared at the barn in the picture on the wall.

"I don't suppose you're wiping away tears of grief with that wadded-up toilet paper."

"Not hardly."

"My granddaddy had a barn just like that."

"Did your granddaddy have a rip in his ass?"

"It could have been worse, Cathy. It could have been from the riverfront slasher!"

Cathy reached over and patted Jack's side. "I wish it were. That means I'd be married to a rich TV star, not a poor, wounded, lost-in-time Confederate".

The Gate

Hazel Grisby and Cora Pickle had not spoken to each other in twenty-seven years. Their family couldn't believe that two sisters could go that long being angry and not having any communication at all. It was a little thing, not a big thing, that pulled them apart, but little things seem to fester in some people's minds and this sore had become a huge boil on Hazel and Cora's butt of dissension.

The dispute went back to when the girls were fifteen and sixteen years of age. Each Sunday their father would hitch up the buggy and mule so the sisters could take a nice ride in the countryside around Bell Buckle. The sisters loved this since they could flirt with the young boys sitting on old wooden benches downtown. Cora was the more prim and proper of the two. Maybe it was because she was the older one, but mainly she was more introverted than Hazel. Hazel let her hair and neckline down and showed more leg than Cora ever thought of.

One Sunday after church and their noon meal, Cora and Hazel went on their usual buggy ride around the countryside, and it was late in the afternoon when they approached the old gate that led into the barnyard. Each Sunday the sisters would take turns getting out of the buggy and opening the gate. That afternoon when the sisters returned home, the mule-drawn buggy stopped as it had done so many times before.

Cora, holding on to the reins, turned to Hazel and said, "It's your turn to open the gate."

Hazel, fiddling with her long hair, said, "No, Cora, it's your turn to open the gate."

"I opened the gate last Sunday, Hazel."

"No you didn't, Cora; I opened the gate last Sunday."

"Hazel, I distinctly remember opening the gate because I got mud on my new shoes."

"No, Cora, that was two weeks ago you got mud on your new

shoes. If you remember correctly, you got mud on your new shoes when you went out to the mailbox."

"I did not go out to the mailbox in my new shoes, and besides, it's you that runs out to the mailbox every day looking for a letter from Charlie Pittman who's gone off and promised he'd write you every day, and you've not received the first envelope."

Hazel, getting more aggravated, snatched off her flower-brimmed hat and said, "Cora, you're just jealous 'cause no one's writing you. Now, get out and open the gate; it's your turn."

"Hazel, if we have to sit here all night, I'm not getting out of this buggy. It's your turn and that's that!"

Cora and Hazel sat in front of the gate until Sam Bailey, who helped around the farm, noticed the girls sitting in the buggy and offered to open the gate. The gate opened but shut off any communication between the girls. Hazel went to her room and Cora went to hers, and they did not speak. Meals became difficult since that had always been a time of joy and talking in the Milligan household. Their parents tried to bridge the gap between their daughters, but it was to no avail. The sisters sat beside each other in the house, church, and school, but not one word was uttered between them.

Each went on to marry and raise a family. Cora married a merchant from Bell Buckle, and Hazel married an insurance salesman and moved to Memphis, Tennessee. Relatives did everything to try to get the girls back together, but not even the deaths of their mama and daddy would resolve the dispute. The girls sat on opposite sides in the church at their parents' funerals. At each service, the preacher talked about how important family was. Everybody thought surely the sisters would speak, but still they refused.

Springs turned to summers, and summers to winters, and the sisters started to realize that they had forfeited a big part of their lives. Cora's children were grown and married and had moved on, leaving her and her husband, Bill, alone in the big old farmhouse that had belonged to Cora's parents. Hazel's one son had been killed in an automobile accident in Arkansas, and her husband had left her for a younger woman. As the sisters grew older, they realized it was time to forgive and forget. Cora and Bill were auctioning off the homeplace where she and her sister had grown up. Their parents had left them both the farm, but since the sisters were not speaking, they never really settled the estate, so Bill and Cora stayed on for years at the farm. But now they were getting older and decided to move to a smaller house in town, for it suited their needs more than the big, old drafty house in which they lived. Cora finally broke down and called Hazel to come home and get any of the furnishings that she might want to keep. Hazel was ready to let go of the farm since she really didn't need it and could always use the money; however, she did want to get the antique clock that had belonged to her grandfather and the cherry jelly cabinet that sat in the large kitchen. She was happy to receive Cora's call, for she knew they were getting older and needed to make up.

Cora remembered that Hazel loved carrot cake and baked one the night before she was to arrive. Bill watched her stew around the kitchen that night. "You think your sister's gonna be happy with us getting rid of a lot of this furniture?"

"I'm sure it'll be OK. She'd like to keep a few pieces, and that's fine with me. After all, we can't use a lot of this since the house we're moving to is so much smaller. Our children don't care anything about the furniture, so I guess we'll sell most of it when we auction off the house."

Bill folded up the evening paper and said, "I'm going to bed; my back is hurting."

Cora glanced over and in a tone of "I told you so" said, "You shouldn't have picked up those heavy boxes at work."

Bill smiled and thought to himself, "Lord, she's always telling me something."

Cora got up early the next morning and made sure the house

was tidy for Hazel's arrival that afternoon. She wondered how they would react when they saw each other. Would they still be strangers, or would blood wash away the years and let them pick up their lives as sisters again?

Trees by the roadside flew by like memories as Hazel drove from Memphis to Bell Buckle. She thought of childhood and all the wonderful times that she and Cora had had when they were children. They had missed out on so much of their adult life. It was around dusk when Hazel pulled into the long drive that led to the old farmhouse where they had grown up. She visualized her daddy walking down the lane to the milk barn and her mama cooking on the old wood stove in the kitchen.

Cora heard the tires on the gravel and ran to the front porch. Hazel parked the car, and with open arms, started toward the front porch. Cora, also with arms open, started down the porch stairs to greet her sister. Both hugged for a long time as tears washed away the years. Finally, Cora let go and said, "Look at you, Hazel. Why, you haven't changed a day."

"Now, Cora, you know I don't look like I did back then, but you are looking more and more like mama."

Cora, wiping away tears, said, "I wish mama could be here."

"She is here, Cora. She's in me, and she's in you, and she's in our hearts."

Cora and Hazel walked up the front porch steps into the old house. Cora straightened a picture on the wall and said, "She's sure in this old house. Sometimes when I'm in the kitchen, I feel her standing over me and saying, 'Don't put too much salt on the roast.' That's what I fixed for your supper tonight, Hazel. I remembered how much you loved mama's roast and her carrot cake."

"Cora, I hope you didn't go to a lot of trouble now, fixing a big supper and all."

"Lord, no, I always fix supper for Bill, and I just added another plate."

Hazel took a deep breath in her mama's kitchen. The old house smelled just like it did years ago. The aroma of supper mingled with cedar closets, burning hickory logs, peppermint candy that was always in the cut-glass dish in the living room, lingering lavender sachet in the opened bureau, and Old English polish that had built up on the banister and dining room table. She heard the same sounds that she heard years before: dishes clanging when taken from the cupboards, wind pushing the front porch swing against the house, uneven poplar floor boards squeaking when she walked, the popping of fire hitting the screen on the hearth. So many sounds that she had missed. Hazel ran her hand down the arm of the wingback chair her daddy always sat in. She touched the eyes on the old cookstove in the kitchen. She brushed her fingers over the cherry chest of drawers in the bedroom. She felt the face of the grandfather clock in the hall. She touched everything that made the house human. However, it was the sight and touch of her sister and the sound of their speaking that brought Hazel home.

Supper was about on the table when Bill got home. Cora pulled the roast out of the oven and said, "Just like mama made, Hazel. You know how we always liked it thick. I can't stand it when they slice a roast. It should be cooked until it falls to pieces in chunks."

Bill took off his coat and hat and extended his hand to Hazel. Hazel laughed and said, "Don't I get a hug? After all, you're married to my sister. That makes us kin."

Bill laughed and felt relieved that everything was going great and no one was having to walk on egg shells. He pulled out a kitchen chair for Hazel.

"No, not that one, Bill; Hazel always sat next to daddy. Put her there next to you."

"Your sister always makes sure everyone sits in the right seat."

"Any chair will do; it's just so great being home."

After the blessing and thanking God for the reunion, Cora

said, "Pass the roast to Hazel."

Hazel pulled a big helping to her plate. Cora, picking up a bowl of mashed potatoes, said, "Hope these mashed potatoes are mashed enough for you. People just don't take the time to whip them right. I like chunks in my beef, but I like my potatoes smooth. Good butter, that's the answer. That's what makes them good and creamy. What about you, Hazel, did you ever learn to cook?"

"Not really; I managed, but I couldn't get it together like this."

"Well, it's not easy. Men think we just snap our fingers and it all falls into place. I'd gladly trade places with Bill. I could run the store and let him run the house. 'Course, we'd starve to death, wear dirty clothes and live in a filthy house."

Hazel looked over at Bill. "I don't think she has much confidence in your housekeeping."

"Oh, I'm used to her fussing; we're getting a smaller house. That should cut down on a lot of her work."

"What Bill doesn't realize is that it takes just the same amount of time and effort to cook three meals in a small kitchen as it does in a big kitchen."

"Now, Cora, Hazel didn't come here to hear us fuss over meals."

"We're not fussing, just discussing. Just like we did all those years at this same old kitchen table. That's why we're eating in the kitchen instead of the dining room. Hazel loved this old kitchen table."

"Cora, we've missed so much. I never got to know your children, and now they're grown and gone."

"You know children. They can't wait to get away from home, then call every other day needing something. I'm so sorry you lost your son in that accident. It must be terrible."

"I try not to think about it, Cora. It left a big hole in my heart. I think that's why Jack left me for a younger woman. He wanted another child, and I was too old to start another family."

"Are you all right, Hazel, money and all? Pass the cornbread, Bill."

"Yes, Cora, I got the house and it was paid for, and I have a job. I'm doing OK."

"Bill, you're putting too much gravy on your potatoes. I swear, Hazel, he just drowns everything in gravy."

Hazel reached for the green beans, and said, "Daddy sure liked gravy and molasses. Remember how he'd always put molasses on his biscuit for dessert?"

"I miss daddy so much, Hazel. He always knew the answer to everything. Well, the answer to everything but us. He went to his grave hoping we'd make up."

"I know, Cora; I wish we hadn't waited so long. There's so many years to catch up on."

"It'll take years to catch up, and I want to hear everything, Hazel. What you've done through all these years. What it's like to live in the big city. I always wanted to stay in that Peabody Hotel in Memphis. Have you ever stayed there?"

"Once. One winter the electricity went off for three days in our neighborhood. Jack and I stayed there, but it doesn't hold good memories for me. That's where Jack met the woman he left me for. She was working the reception desk in the restaurant."

"Goodness, I'm sorry I brought it up."

"That's OK, Cora, I've had time to heal, and I sure don't want a man who doesn't want me."

A sudden thought came to Cora. "You know Charlie Pittman never did marry. He just lives about three miles from here. I can call him and tell him you've come home."

"Lord, Cora, that crush was twenty-seven years ago. I've forgotten he ever existed. Besides, I don't need another man in my life. I'm enjoying being by myself."

"You always liked to be by yourself. You'd go to your room when you were a little girl and play by yourself. I used to wonder what in the world you were doing in there."

"Reading, Cora. I loved to read, and I pretended I was the main character in every book."

"You always had an adventurous soul. Bill, one time she rode the train over to the next town. Mama and daddy worried to death when she didn't come home. We never dreamed she slipped into mama's egg money and bought herself a train ticket. Daddy had to drive over to Murfreesboro and get her. It's a good thing mama didn't have much money in her lard tin. Lord, Hazel would've ended up in Chicago, or Heaven knows where.

"Cora, you're just jealous, 'cause you never misbehaved. You always did everything mama and daddy wanted you to do."

"Twenty-seven years, Hazel, twenty-seven years. Here we are, sitting at the kitchen table like old times. What were we thinking?"

"I don't know, Cora, just young girls not thinking right. It was a silly argument, and we both were immature."

"Thank God, we're older now, and can use good judgment. Those old buggy days are far behind us, Hazel."

"I miss them, Cora; life was so simple then, taking a Sunday afternoon ride around Bell Buckle. It seems like a million years ago."

"Oh, I remember it like it was yesterday, us sitting there, me holding those reins, and you twisting your hair."

"How long did we sit there, Cora?"

"Several hours, Hazel. If old Sam hadn't showed up, I guess we'd still be sitting there."

"Whatever happened to old Sam?"

"He died about fifteen years ago, had a stroke in his sleep. I guess if you have to go, that's the way, in your sleep. I can still see him around the farm helping daddy run the place."

"Whatever happened to that old buggy, Cora?"

"Daddy sold it years ago. He said it reminded him too much of our foolishness."

"We were foolish, Cora. Not speaking all these years over a

little thing."

Cora picked up the dessert plate and passed the carrot cake to Hazel. "I know, Hazel, it was over a little thing, but it *was* your turn to open the gate."

Hallow's Eve

Spunk Spurlock had a hankering for reading, especially when he was constipated. That's why he kept his *Popular Mechanics, Field and Stream,* and *Hunt and Gun* magazines in an orange crate between the shower stall and commode. A couple of times a day Spunk would journey into his reading room and turn through the yellowing pages, admiring the pretty colored pictures that to his mind enhanced the creativity of the articles. On constipated days, Spunk managed to thumb through several magazines, then he would count the swans on the torn paper hanging on the bathroom walls.

Spunk lived in the small town of Bell Buckle, Tennessee. Townsfolk knew he wasn't bright, but then again he wasn't really retarded, so they just called him slow. Bell Buckle had a population of 453, if everybody was at home. Downtown was a half square with buildings that had survived the rages of time and weather. On the left side of the square, there was a dry goods store run by Mr. John Bunker. Mr. Bunker let Spunk sweep up in the afternoons so he could make picture-show money.

It didn't take much for Spunk to live on. His parents had both died and had left him a small house and ten acres just on the outside of town. Spunk kept a garden, and with his love for hunting and fishing, he managed to keep food on the table all year. Now and then townsfolk would bring him pies and cakes and hot buttered biscuits left over from Sunday dinners. Spunk was always obliged and loved the people of Bell Buckle.

When Spunk turned thirty-seven in August, Mr. Bunker gave him a surprise birthday party down at Bunker's Dry Goods. Nearly everybody from town showed up and brought Spunk a present. His favorite was the powder horn that Bernard Conwell gave him. Mr. Conwell said it had belonged to Spunk's great-great-grandaddy, and he should have it. Spunk asked Mr. Conwell how he had come by it, and Mr. Conwell said that his

81

grandfather had won it playing horseshoes.

Spunk never played horseshoes much, but he had them hanging all around the house for good luck. He placed almost as much power in the horseshoes as he did in the rabbit's foot in his pants pocket. Spunk wouldn't go anyplace without that hairy rabbit's foot. He had shot the white-tail when he was a young boy. The rabbit's foot was about the proudest thing he owned. Spunk had lots of fur around. Every year he would switch the squirrel's tail on the antenna of his 1952 Ford pickup. He kept the old tails in a bureau drawer in the living room. Once Essie Johnson opened the drawer and had to be treated in the next town's emergency room. Even today, people say Miss Essie wakes up in the night screaming and swatting at furry things.

One fall morning a Jehovah's Witness, not finding Spunk at home, left a pamphlet in the mailbox. Somehow, the pamphlet accidentally got slipped into the October edition of *Field and Stream*. That afternoon Spunk crossed the gravel road, picked up his mail out of the plow mailbox, and slowly made his way back to the house. He placed his new reading material on the orange crate. That evening after supper, Spunk retired to his favorite reading spot and picked up his newly-arrived magazine. The pictures of deer and wild hogs took him into a world of make-believe.

Suddenly, Spunk became a big game hunter. He imagined his walls covered with heads of lions, tigers, and elephants. He could see big white tusks lying on his hearth. He especially loved the head of the antelope that he had killed in Africa. He had it protruding from the wall near the front door, and there he hung his Caterpillar hat on the largest antler.

As Spunk continued looking at the pictures, all of a sudden he noticed the pamphlet inside the magazine. He had never seen this before but figured he was getting something extra in this issue. After all, it was getting close to Christmas, and *Field and Stream* was probably pushing a gift subscription for a friend. Slowly

Spunk's eyes and finger followed the print. "Halloween is a sin and follows the occult. It derives from the pagan days of Hallow's Eve: a time to drive off the evil spirits, a time of super-stitions when people used scarecrows and pumpkins to scare off the evil lurking about. Those who participate in such pagan ritu-als will be damned to Hell." The pamphlet went on to say that we are in the "last days" and that the signs are all around. Spunk thought it unusual for *Field and Stream* to be talking about such things, but if *Field and Stream* said it, it must be so. Now Spunk was truly troubled. It was three days to Halloween, and he needed to search his soul, for Halloween had always been his favorite holiday. Every year Mr. Bunker would try to convince Spunk that Halloween was not a recognized holiday for time off, but every October 31st Spunk took off from his sweeping all the same. He still got a thrill wearing his bed sheet once a year.

Suddenly Spunk put down the magazine and pulled up his pants, went straight to the woodshed, got an ax, and returned to his front yard. He wasn't about to go to Hell, especially if the end was near. He remembered all the terrible things he had learned about Hell from his mama. He wasn't about to burn in no lake of fire. Repeatedly lowering the ax, Spunk squashed all the pump-kins he had carved and placed on the rotten fence posts. He walked onto his front porch and ripped down the cardboard skeleton hanging on the front door. How could he have gone all these years and not known Halloween was from the devil? He sat down in his front porch rocking chair, a large, five-ladderback with two slats missing. He remembered just two nights before he had seen a musical group on his black and white TV and had thought then that they looked like they had come straight out of the bottom of Hell. How could a place like America let demons into the homes of innocent people? It's them big city folk from New York, he figured. They don't know a demon from an Eskimo Pie. No wonder the country was in the shape it was in.

Why, just last week he'd been in Smutt's Record Shop searching for his favorite Ernest Tubb record. While looking for Tubb's "Walking the Floor Over You," he'd passed a counter full of albums. On the front covers were bats, snakes, and people dressed like vampires. Good Lord, he remembered that Revelations had mentioned that albums would look like this before the end of time. *Field and Stream* was right. Even Smutt's Record Shop was promoting the occult, whatever that was.

Over the next few nights, Spunk ate all the trick-or-treat candy himself. He wanted no part of Halloween. A few days later, he was preparing for Halloween by not preparing. Just after dark on Halloween night, Rodney Scruggs, Leonard Simpson, and Felix Patterson appeared at Spunk's front door. All three had dressed for the occasion. Felix had cut the bottom out of a large tin garbage can and held it up with baling wire. On his head was a galvanized bedpan. Rodney had painted skeletons on his over-alls, and Leonard had come in a box with chicken feathers pasted all over it. Normally, Spunk would have been on the front porch waiting for the boys, but this time he was not in his usual place. Leonard yelled, "Come on, Spunk! You ready?"

"Not going," was the answer that came from behind the rusty screen door.

"Whatcha mean, not going? You sick or something?"

"I said I ain't going!"

"Why not? Who smashed all the pumpkins? Someone been here 'fore us?"

"I smashed 'em."

"You smashed 'em! Good Lord, Spunk, why did you go and do a thing like that?"

"It ain't right. Halloween ain't right. You boys git on now. Have your fun somewhere else."

Rodney, Felix, and Leonard pushed the front screen door open and found Spunk in his favorite living room rocking chair, a wine velvet platform rocker with one arm broken. Spunk was staring at the fire he had made. The sound of popping hickory helped hypnotize him and took his mind off the fun he had always had on this night.

"What's the matter, Spunk? What's your sheet still doing on your bed?"

"I told you for the last time, I ain't going."

"You mad at us or something?"

"I ain't mad; now just leave me be!"

Puzzled, the three boys left Spunk's living room and returned to the front yard.

"I can't believe Spunk ain't going," Leonard said as he pulled out his buck knife and scraped the blade against his cheek.

"He's acting mighty strange," said Rodney, as he bent down to tie the string on his brogan.

"You reckon he's going through the change? I hear men go through it, too. They say you do strange things. Spunk's acting strange; he's gone with us on Halloween for years."

"Good Lord, Leonard, Spunk was born strange," said Rodney.

"I bet that's it! Spunk's going through the change, whatever that is," said Felix.

"What do you know, Felix? You're only eight years old and ain't done nothing or been nowhere," quipped Rodney in his authoritative voice.

"Well, you're eighteen, and I don't see no big-ass diploma hanging on your wall."

"Don't you smart mouth me, Felix, or I'll take that bedpan off your head and shove it where the sun don't shine; then you'll doo doo in style."

"All right, you two," said Leonard. "We ain't gonna find out anything fighting amongst us."

"Maybe he's in love," said Felix.

"Who in the world would be dumb enough to be in love with Spunk?" laughed Rodney.

"I'll bet you my buck knife against your pocket watch, Rodney, that Spunk's got a woman."

Felix's eyes lit up. "She'd have to be as dumb as Spunk. Reckon there's a woman dumb as him?"

"I don't know, but I've seen that look before," said Leonard.

"What look, Leonard?"

"That look Spunk had when he was staring at the fireplace; I saw that look once when pa thought ma had run off with the milk truck man."

"I never knew your ma run off with no milk driver," said Rodney.

"She didn't. She just got aggravated with pa and went to her sister's. Poor old pa stared at that fire all night, right sick looking, just like Spunk's doing now. Sitting in that old living room and staring into the blamed fire."

"Maybe Leonard's right, Rodney. Spunk looks mighty sheepish. It takes love to make a man look sheepish."

Rodney looked over at Leonard and, in almost a hush, said, "You reckon Spunk's ever done it?"

"Done what?" asked Felix.

Rodney and Leonard looked at Felix. "Done it with a woman."

Rodney then turned and said, "'Course, Leonard, I bet you ain't done it, neither."

"How you know so much, Rodney?"

"'Cause you're thirteen and you still got pimples."

"What's pimples got to do with it?"

"They clear up when you do it."

"Well, maybe I ain't done it yet, but I'm going to!"

"When?" Rodney snickered.

"When I get ready."

"When he's ready. Hear that, Felix? When he's ready. Reckon that'll be when he's dry behind the ears."

"Quit making fun of Leonard, Rodney. I ain't seen women falling all over you, except that Willa Mae, and she falls over ever'body."

Felix interrupted the argument by announcing, "My daddy

done it this morning."

"How you know?"

"'Cause this morning at the breakfast table, my daddy turned over his molasses on his biscuits, and mama said, 'Now you done it.'"

The screen door slammed, and Spunk was on the front porch. "Get on out of here. I told you not to be hanging 'round here tonight."

All three boys walked part way up to the front porch.

"You in love, Spunk?" asked Leonard.

"What you talking 'bout?"

"The way you was sitting staring at the fire. We kinda figured you got a girl."

"I ain't got no girl."

"Then maybe that's what's wrong, Spunk. You need a girl."

"Don't want one. Happy the way I am."

"Then what is it, Spunk? This ain't like you. You always said this was your favorite holiday. Every year you gone with us and turned over Morgan Cox's outhouse. One year he was in it, you remember?"

"I ain't turning over no outhouse."

Rodney walked up on the porch, put his arm around Spunk, and whispered, "Your hunting dog ain't run off with the milkman, has he?"

A short distance away they all heard the small voices of children. Slowly, the sight of skeletons, vampires, ghosts, and goblins neared the porch. They each carried pumpkin lanterns and sacks for treats.

"Trick or treat!"

By this time Spunk was getting very annoyed. "There ain't no treats here. Get out of my yard!"

The children looked and listened in disbelief. Spunk had always been their friend. They looked forward to his Tootsie Rolls each year.

Leonard turned to the small children and said, "You'd better listen; Spunk ain't in no good mood."

The goblin spoke up, "Mr. Spunk, you always got us candy. Look, we even brung you a plastic pumpkin. You can use it all year long. I'm sure you got us our Tootsie Rolls."

"Got nothing. You children go somewhere else. Leonard, Felix, Rodney, I'll see you tomorrow. Go on now, take your devilment somewhere else."

It was no use. Everyone had to leave Spunk behind while they traveled off into the night. Spunk watched them walk down the narrow road until their voices were out of range. It was painful for Spunk. This year the outhouse would not be turned over by him.

He returned to his fire and rocking chair but not before he turned all the lights out. No one would come to the porch with the lights out. Spunk rocked and thought and watched the fire flicker. How could *Field and Stream* be so mean? All through the years the magazine had brought him nothing but joy. But now, it was telling him Halloween was of the devil.

Spunk thought about all the years he had gone trick-or-treating with the boys. He remembered the funny costumes his mama had made him when he was a little boy. Spunk rocked and tried to get it out of his mind when all of a sudden a deep thought occurred to him. If Halloween is of the devil, then the other holidays might not be right either. He thought about the spirit of Santa Claus. Not Santa Claus! Surely not Santa Claus. It was Santa Claus who had brought Spunk that Browning automatic shotgun he cherished. It still looked like new. He got it when he was fourteen years old, and he watched over it like it was a baby. He cleaned the barrel every day and polished the wood to a high gloss.

Slowly, Spunk got up from his chair and went to the orange crate, then he returned to the living room closet where he kept his Browning automatic. In his left hand he held the magazine; in his right hand he gripped the gun. They both lay heavy upon his heart. The left hand was telling Spunk the right hand was wrong. Spunk walked to the fireplace balancing each hand. It was more than he could take. His life had revolved around hunting. Slowly he ran his fingers over the initials that were carved on the butt of his precious shotgun. He had no choice. It would be Hell here if he could not hunt.

With a quick flip of the wrist, Spunk tossed the magazine into the fire. He ran to the closet and placed the gun against the closet wall so it would be safe. His thoughts turned to how mean he had been to those little children. They had gone away from his yard without one Tootsie Roll. Spunk couldn't take it anymore. He grabbed the sheet off his bed, ran down the road to find the boys, and later that night turned over Mr. Cox's outhouse.

The next day Spunk canceled his subscription to *Field and Stream*.

Cedar By The Window

Yazoo City was a yazoo town. Like so many small southern towns, it no longer satisfied the grown southern boy who had returned from the war. Parker Bowman had spent his entire life in Mississippi, but now he was restless and not sure of what the future held.

Carrie Ruth, Parker's sister, really didn't think about the future. The closest she got to the war was a Betty Grable movie at the local picture show. For her, the Second World War meant romance, song and dance. She did pay attention to the short newsreels before the feature film, hoping to see her brother among the many men that were fighting for their country. Once she could have sworn that she saw Parker waving to her, but then again, in uniform they all looked alike to her.

Sunday evenings had always been family time in the Bowman household. They all gathered by the radio to hear their favorite show, and now that Parker had returned from the war things were back to normal. Carrie Ruth stood by the open window fingering the string pull of the living room shade. Parker sat in the overstuffed red velvet chair by the Philco radio. Slowly the evening paper dropped down to his lap. "Good heavens, Carrie Ruth, quit fiddling with that window shade. It's getting on my nerves."

Carrie Ruth bounced the pull off the window. "I hate the wind when it comes out of the southeast. It brings that awful smell of Bobby Metcalf's dairy barn right into our living room."

Worn out with it all, Parker snapped, "A little manure smell never hurt anyone. Besides, if it bothers you that much, turn on the fan."

"Turning on the fan just spreads it around more."

"Well, write a letter to God; you write to everyone else complaining. 'Dear God: You must stop the southeast wind; it makes my living room smell like manure.'"

"Don't you be sacrilegious, Parker Bowman."

91

Henry Bowman could hear his squabbling children from the adjacent room. He knew they needed a referee; they usually did when they got into it.

"What's this yelling about?"

"Just smell, Daddy. Take a deep breath."

Henry filled his lungs and held his breath for a moment.

"Well, what do you smell?"

"October. God, I love October."

Parker rose and handed his dad the evening paper. He turned to his sister and said, "See, the smell is in the nose of the beholder."

"You can't even be original, Parker Bowman, and if your nose wasn't so bent out of joint all the time, you could smell it, too."

Parker sat down on the sofa and let his daddy have the big overstuffed chair.

"Carrie Ruth is writing a letter to God about Bobby Metcalf's dairy farm. She's torn between writing Congress or God since she's not sure who's in control of the wind."

Carrie Ruth yanked the shade down. "While I'm writing my letter, I might mention the smell of your hair. I don't know which is worse, cow manure or your Wild Root Creme Oil."

Henry Bowman folded the paper. "Now, now. It's Sunday night; let's see if we can have a nice, enjoyable evening."

"Forget the letter, Carrie Ruth," said Parker. "I forgot it's God's day off."

"Parker, you need to have more respect, don't he, Daddy? Ever since he got back from the war he's been acting this way."

"Parker was gone a long time, Carrie Ruth. He saw a bigger world than you and I have ever seen. Maybe he is a little bored coming back home to a small town."

"I'm not bored, Daddy–well, maybe a little bored, but I'm glad to be home. Wherever I was overseas I thought of home thousands of times. Why, I could smell Bobby Metcalf's barn all over Europe. I guess I just sometimes get upset with Carrie Ruth for complaining all the time."

"Well, someone's got to complain. Why, Senator Bilbo personally wrote me a letter on his Washington stationery and thanked me for my thoughts on war rationing."

Henry Bowman turned toward Parker and smiled. "Your sister thought everybody should grow sugar cane in his back yard."

The evening confrontation was interrupted when Mary Bowman entered the room with chocolate cake. "It's almost time for Jack Benny. Is anybody watching the clock?"

"I've been too busy separating your offspring."

Mary placed the chocolate cake and napkins on the table. "Henry, that tie looks awful on you."

Henry turned to Parker and winked. "Carrie Ruth took after her mother."

"Surely you didn't wear that tie to church this morning. I sat next to you for an hour, but I don't remember what tie you had on. But I believe I'd remember if you wore that awful thing."

"Mary, you gave me this tie last Christmas."

Mary took a closer look. "Last Christmas I had poor judgment. Besides, I have an excuse for not thinking right last Christmas; our son wasn't here. How awful it must be to spend Christmas away from home. I had to mail the packages three months before December to make sure you got them, son. And I had to knit your sweater two months before that to make sure it would be finished."

"It was a beautiful sweater, Mom."

Henry pulled his pocket watch out. "It's nearly time for Jack Benny."

Parker turned on the old Philco and started to adjust the dial. "Someday we'll see him. They've got this box that looks like a radio only you see pictures."

Carrie Ruth almost dropped her cake. "You mean to tell me we'll sit here and just look at the radio?"

Henry wiped his mouth with a napkin. "Parker is right. I read that they are experimenting in New York with these pictures through the air. I would just like to see Walter Winchell. Lord, I love Winchell."

Henry stood and started to imitate Winchell. "'Good evening, Mr. and Mrs. America and all the ships at sea–let's go to press.' Oh, how I would love to see him say that."

Mary patted her husband on the back. "Quit dreaming, Henry, it won't be in your lifetime."

"Yes, it will, Mama," said Parker. "Why, men will go to the moon in daddy's lifetime."

Parker's mother cut her eyes to Carrie Ruth. "I'm beginning to think that Carrie Ruth is right, Parker. Maybe the war did affect your mind."

"It didn't affect my mind, Mama. At least, not the way you're thinking."

Carrie Ruth brushed chocolate cake crumbs from her lap onto her napkin. "If God had meant us to be on the moon then he would have put us there."

Parker jumped up. "Boy, I'm glad you weren't Queen Isabella, Carrie Ruth. I can see you telling Columbus now, 'Well, if God had meant for us to be on the other side of the world, he'd of put us there.'"

Carrie Ruth stood and put her hands on her hips. "That's different. Columbus was only crossing the sea."

Parker pointed to the ceiling. "What do you think is out there? Space is the sea only without water."

"You're right: hot air just like you, Parker Bowman."

"Let's stop this nonsense," snapped Mary Bowman. "All this talk about pictures on the radio and men on the moon; I do well to know how the can opener works."

A knock on the door interrupted the conversation. Henry greeted John Cantrell, long-time friend of the family. Cantrell was a man in his sixties and seemed always to know what was going on in the neighborhood. The Bowmans could expect him to show up any time there was news, good or bad.

"Hello, Henry. I hope I'm not disturbing you and your family."

"Not at all. Quite the contrary, your timing is perfect. A few more minutes Carrie Ruth and Parker might have qualified for the lightweight championship."

John Cantrell extended his hand to Parker. "I should have stopped in before now to say hello and welcome you home from the army, but I've been to a wedding in Bell Buckle, Tennessee."

"Thank you. It's good to be home." Then turning to Carrie Ruth, Parker mumbled, "I think."

In her usual cheerful way Mary said, "Let me take your coat and you must have a piece of chocolate cake."

"No thank you, Mary," said John. "I can't stay long; I'm on my way to the hospital. My niece had her baby this afternoon, a seven-pound, two-ounce boy."

Mary smiled. "That must make you mighty proud."

"Yes, it doesn't make me feel any younger, but it makes me feel awfully good. They named the boy after me."

Henry put his arm around John. "That's wonderful. The only thing that was ever named after me was Carrie Ruth's turtle."

Mary looked over at Henry. "That was because you were both so slow."

"Like I said, I can only stay a minute, but I wanted to stop in to tell you about old man Tidwell's will."

Ben Tidwell had lived his life next door to the Bowmans. His flowers and birds had become his family. During the day, neighbors could see him cutting the hedge and feeding the birds. His favorite expression was, "God gave birds more sense than He did people." All the neighbors figured Ben Tidwell would leave his belongings to charity, maybe to animals. He always felt sorry for strays. Many times he would nurse a lost kitten back to health and neighbors used to say that Tidwell would spend his last dime on lumber to make birdhouses for his back yard.

Henry turned to John. "I'm going to miss him next door. That yard just doesn't seem right without him out there fooling with his flowers and birds."

Carrie Ruth interrupted, "I don't know why he liked the mockingbirds; they just dive at you every time you go into the yard."

Henry looked at Carrie Ruth. "That's their way of protecting their young. Anyway, back to Mr. Tidwell, he always felt sorry for the underprivileged, so I'm sure his house next door will sell and go to a good cause."

John Cantrell paused and dug at the flower on the carpet with the toe of his shoe. "Well, not exactly; that's what I stopped in about. It seems Tidwell left his home to Jenny and Arthur Bee."

First there was silence, then with the exception of Parker, there was a shout in unison almost like breaking out in song, "Jenny and Arthur Bee!"

"Why, there must be some mistake, John," said Mary. "He couldn't have done that; Arthur and Jenny Bee are colored!"

"Well, Mary, colored or not, they own the house next door," said John.

Carrie Ruth fell down onto the overstuffed velvet chair. "This is awful!"

Henry could not believe his ears, either. "Are you sure, John?"

"Positive. Seems Jenny and Arthur Bee found a warm place in Tidwell's heart. He felt sorry for them being eighty or so and living in that falling-down shanty. Evidently Mr. Tidwell knew he was going to die, and he made his last wish very plain. It's all in writing."

Parker raised his eyebrows. "Hurray for Mr. Tidwell. He's still taking care of the birds and bees."

"Blackbirds!" yelled Carrie Ruth. "Have you gone crazy, Parker Bowman? Our next-door neighbors are going to be colored!"

Mary put her hand behind her and felt for the couch. "Quick, someone, get me a drink of cool water."

Henry patted Mary. "Now, now. It may not be as bad as it

seems."

"As bad as it seems!" yelled Carrie Ruth. "Daddy, we're ruined!"

Mary picked up the evening paper and started to fan. "Henry, did you say anything to make old man Tidwell mad while he was alive? That's what it is, revenge. It must be revenge."

"It's not revenge, Mary," said Henry. "You know how soft-hearted Ben Tidwell was. I'm sure he felt this was his way of doing a good deed."

John Cantrell knew it was exit time. "Like I said, I just dropped in for a moment to tell you the news. Thought you might like to know the situation."

There was a moment of silence when John left. It was like they all were replaying the conversation to make sure they heard it right.

Mary's eyes focused on the funeral home calendar that was hanging on the wall. "Henry, what will we do?"

"Nothing, Mary. What can we do?"

Carrie Ruth pondered and wrung her hands. "Surely we can do something. A petition! That's good. A petition with enough signatures gets things done."

Henry turned to Carrie Ruth. "If the property has been deeded to Arthur and Jenny, then I'm afraid it's theirs."

"This is terrible, Daddy, and Parker, you're just sitting there not saying nothing."

"Good grief, Carrie Ruth. Your great-grandfather had Negroes living next door to him."

"That's because he owned them."

Mary's eyes were still turned toward the funeral calendar. Somehow it brought tranquility to the moment; by changing the subject, she would not have to deal with the problem.

"I remember grandpapa's place. For miles all you saw was cotton. It was like waves coming in on the gulf down around Gulfport and people were always singing. It seems picking cotton had a rhythm and the ones picking it set it to music."

Parker walked over and put his arm around Mary. "You can't spend your life looking back to what was, Mama."

Carrie Ruth wiped the tears from her eyes. "I'll just die. Billy Roy will never ask me to marry him now. I'm ruined for life. I'll be known as the old maid who lived next door to the colored."

"What's this talk of Billy Roy marrying you?" said Henry. "You never mentioned this before."

"This is some of Carrie Ruth's imagination, Daddy. I just saw Billy Roy last week and he sure didn't mention anything about marrying Carrie Ruth, although he was sure upset about something."

"You mean you're thinking about marrying Billy Roy and you haven't even told your mama?"

"Well, Mama, he hasn't exactly asked me yet, but I know he was going to. I think the Fourth of July picnic put the idea in his head. We won the cakewalk, and we just seemed to be natural together, walking and stepping to the music. Our bodies were in perfect time. The judges said they didn't know when they had ever seen a more perfect walk. Ever since then Billy Roy has been paying me a lot of attention and just several days ago he asked me for my ring size. I figured he's going to spring it on me about Christmastime, but he'll never ask me now, Mama."

"Surely if he loves you, your next-door neighbors won't matter."

"Of course they matter, Daddy; they're a stigma. I just hate old man Tidwell. How could he do such a thing? I'm ruined for life."

"You are not ruined for life, Sis. Arthur and Jennie Bee are in their eighties. What possible harm can they bring you? As a matter of fact, they'll probably make better neighbors than Mr. Tidwell. I hear Jennie Bee fixes a mighty mean meal. She'll probably be bringing us food all the time."

"That's all we need!" screamed Carrie Ruth. "The living room smelling like chittlins. Manure on one side and chittlins on the other."

"I've never eaten a chittlin; what are they anyway?"

"Hog guts, Mama, hog guts. We're living next door to people who eat hog guts."

"Oh, my..."

"Like I said before, it may not be as bad as we think," said Henry.

"Oh, Daddy, it's the worst thing that could happen. Fix it; you could always fix everything."

Henry looked at Carrie Ruth with tenderness. "I don't know if I can fix this one, Carrie Ruth."

For the next two weeks, members of the Bowman household spent their time peeking through the window curtains to see what was happening next door. The old furniture that Ben Tidwell left was better than any of Jennie and Arthur Bee's, so they only brought with them special pieces they cherished like the old pie safe Miss Gertrude gave them years ago. It didn't take long for Jennie and Arthur to adjust to their new home. For the first time in many years they wouldn't have to stuff paper through the cracks in the walls to keep warm.

"No use staring out the window, Carrie Ruth. That's not going to make them disappear."

"My God, Parker, they must have forty grandchildren playing in the yard. They don't have babies, they have litters."

"Now, they haven't bothered us in any way. They stay in their own yard. Today, one of the small boys threw a ball, and it landed in our back yard. He wouldn't even come over; I had to throw the ball back myself."

"Well, I still say that they shouldn't be over there. They're good people, but they're just not good enough to live beside us."

"Carrie Ruth, you're my sister and I love you very much and I know you mean well, but I just came from a war where a man five-foot-two thought he was as big as God, so he appointed himself just that. He thought he'd make a better world, so he reached out his hands and his hands became an enormous army that took over towns and countries, and millions of people died because they weren't good enough to be his neighbors."

"That's different, Parker. You're talking about a maniac."

"But it's not different. It's the same principle."

"Parker, I'd never kill anyone, even if he were beneath me."

"I know you wouldn't. I'm not talking about the killing; I'm talking about the hating. Hating is something we learn just like loving is something we learn. It just seems like on a scale hate weighs more."

"I don't hate Jennie and Arthur Bee; I just hate them living next door."

"That's because you feel threatened, Carrie Ruth. As long as their kind stayed on their side of town, they 'knew their place.' Now their place is next to you, and if their physical place gets next to you, then next their social place changes. You're not ready for it; the town is not ready for it, but you cannot hold the black man back, Carrie Ruth. He left the cotton fields over seventy years ago and he'll leave his side of town, too. Arthur and Jennie didn't ask to leave their side of town and live next to us. It's a sign of coming times, brother helping brother."

"But it ain't right to call a colored man brother. If God had created him to be my brother, he'd have created him white like in God's own image."

"Like His own image? What makes you think God is white?"

"Why, of course He is."

"Carrie Ruth, God is not a white Anglo-Saxon. God created everyone. When the Bible says, 'God created man in his own image,' it wasn't talking about color or shape of eyes or anything that makes up the physical form of man. A Chinese sees God as a Chinese, a black man sees Him as black, a white sees Him as white, Catholics see Him as Catholic, Jews see Him as a Jew. It depends on whose eyes you're looking through. The truth is, we shouldn't look for Him with our eyes; we should see Him through our hearts. That's what His image is: love, kindness, forgiveness. That's the image that He made us in."

Carrie Ruth noticed a car pull into the driveway. "Lord, Parker, here comes Billy Roy and Will. I hope you don't do any philosophizing tonight. 'Specially trying to tell me how God scooped up the earth and made us in His own image. How in the world did you get all of that from a handful of dirt?"

Parker met Billy Roy and Will at the door. "Billy Roy, we were just talking about you: how nice and sweet and good-looking you are," said Carrie Ruth.

Will shook hands with Parker. "Well, weren't you saying anything about me, Carrie Ruth?"

"We were about to when you knocked on the door."

Carrie Ruth took Billy Roy by the arm and directed him to the couch. "Come on and sit down. Mama just made some homemade peach ice cream."

Will stood with his hands in his pockets feeling a little uncomfortable. "I hope you didn't mind my coming with Billy Roy, but Jeanette is out of town visiting her grandparents, and I thought it'd be a good chance to visit with some old friends."

"Of course we don't mind," said Parker. "Besides, Will, I haven't seen you since I got home. It's a good chance for us to catch up on everything."

"Well, Parker, there's not much catching up 'cause there ain't much happening around here."

"But things sure have happened in this neighborhood," blurted out Carrie Ruth.

"So I've heard. How are your new neighbors?"

Parker interrupted, "Lord, Will, don't get her started."

"We're not going to talk about neighbors or war," said Carrie Ruth.

The four of them sat down, laughed and joked and ate homemade peach ice cream. Parker noticed that Billy Roy had dropped his spoon a couple of times and remembered that Billy

Roy was acting nervously the last time he saw him at the drugstore. "Are you OK, Billy Roy?"

"Yes, I'm fine, Parker."

Will was on his third bowl of ice cream. "This sure is good homemade ice cream."

Carrie Ruth looked at Will. "The secret is Junket. You've got to use Junket."

"Did you make this ice cream, Carrie Ruth?"

"Why, Billy Roy, I can make anything–pies, cakes, biscuits, and my green beans always win a ribbon at the county fair."

Will nudged Billy Roy. "She's a good cook, Billy Roy."

Nervously Billy Roy answered, "Yes, I know."

Will turned to Parker. "I guess you have a lot of stories about the war you could tell us."

"I've had enough of the war, Will, so let's talk of more pleasant things."

"I'm glad I didn't have to go; I guess I was just lucky. Boy, were you lucky, Billy Roy, color blindness kept you home."

"I wanted to go, Will. I felt it my duty to go. I don't see how color blindness could have made a difference."

"Well, don't get so upset," said Will.

"I'm sorry, I just have something on my mind bothering me."

Carrie Ruth took the bowl from Billy's hand and set it on the coffee table.

"What on earth could be on your mind, Billy Roy? The war is over, it's a few months till Christmas, and you're with me eating homemade peach ice cream."

"I wish I could tell you, Carrie Ruth; it's just I can't."

"What in the world could be so bad that you can't tell me?"

"I wish I could. I just wish I could."

Parker looked over at Carrie Ruth. "If Billy Roy doesn't want to discuss it, Carrie Ruth, don't push him."

"I'm not pushing him; I just always heard that if you have a problem and you tell someone it helps."

"Carrie Ruth's right," said Will. "Billy Roy, if you've got a problem, we'll listen. Lord, we've all got problems."

"It's just awful. I wish I could tell someone. Lord, I need to tell someone, but it's just too awful."

"You haven't murdered anybody, have you?"

"It's worse than that, Carrie Ruth."

"Worse than that? How could anything be worse than that?"

"There are things worse; it's just that I can't talk about them."

"Well, I remember one night overseas to take our minds off how scared we were, we all told something on ourselves, something we might not want someone else to know. It took our minds off what was going on, and it got us through an awful night. Maybe that's what we can do here. We can all tell something on ourselves that no one else would know and which we might not want known. That way, Billy Roy, you could say what's bothering you 'cause we'd all be telling something on ourselves."

Carrie Ruth's eyes lit up. "It would be our own little secrets. Parker, that's the smartest thing you've said since you've been home, and I'm for anything that will help Billy Roy from being so nervous."

Will jumped to his feet and said, "I'll even go first. When I was thirteen, I stole a baseball glove from the five-and-dime. I never told anybody."

Carrie Ruth glanced around the living room. "Goodness, you're not still thieving, are you?"

"Aw, come on, Will. Is that the worst thing you've ever done?" asked Parker.

"That's the worst thing. What about you, Parker? What have you done?"

"Well, I guess the one thing no one knows is that in 1940 I voted for Wendell Wilkie."

Carrie Ruth jumped to her feet. "Wendell Wilkie! Wendell Wilkie! Not only am I living next door to colored, I'm living in a house with a Republican!"

"And all *I* did was steal a glove," smiled Will.

"It's not necessarily that I'm a Republican, Carrie Ruth; it's just that Franklin Roosevelt had already spent two terms as president. Besides, Wilkie supported Roosevelt's foreign policy and favored many of the New Deal programs for social reforms."

"Does daddy know about this?"

"Now, Carrie Ruth, we all promised that our secrets would stay in this room. Besides, I'm not ashamed of it."

"Well, you ought to be," shouted Carrie Ruth. "You're probably the only person in Mississippi that voted Republican."

Parker turned to Billy Roy. "It's your turn, Billy Roy."

"I don't know; it's just awful what I've done. I wish it were just stealing a ball glove or voting for the wrong man. Carrie Ruth, you go next."

"I'll go last; that way I promise that no matter what you tell, Billy Roy, I'll tell something worse."

"Carrie Ruth, you may never speak to me again and that would hurt me so much to know that I've done something to make you ashamed of me."

Carrie Ruth patted Billy Roy's hand. "I couldn't be ashamed of you no matter what it was."

"Well, here goes." Billy Roy looked around the room and in a mumbling voice said, "I did it with a sheep."

"What?" asked Carrie Ruth. "You're mumbling."

Billy Roy shouted, "I did it with a sheep!"

A silence fell over the room. Not the kind of silence of disbelief when they found out the colored family was moving in next door, but the kind of silence that suggests, "I can't believe he just said that."

Eventually Will fell over laughing. Carrie Ruth jumped to her feet, knocking every bowl off the coffee table. "You did what?"

"It's true, Carrie Ruth. I did it with a sheep."

Will managed to straighten himself up. "You're right, Billy Roy. I don't believe you should have told it."

Carrie Ruth eased herself back to the couch. "What on earth would have made you do that?"

Parker reached over and tapped Will on the arm. "Quit laughing, Will. If this is bothering Billy Roy, no one should be laughing. We're playing this game to help him."

Billy Roy looked around. "That's not all; it gets worse."

"What did you do, marry it?" laughed Will.

"I knew I shouldn't have told you. See how you're taking it."

"It's OK, Billy Roy," said Parker, "you're not the first man to do that with a sheep."

"There's something else I did worse than that, Parker."

Carrie Ruth interrupted, "What in the world could be worse than that?"

"Kissing it first," Will said, still holding his sides.

"Would you shut up, Will! This is serious," said Carrie Ruth.

Parker walked over to Billy Roy. "Well, evidently there's more on your mind, and since you've told us this much, tell us the rest."

Billy Roy rubbed his sweaty palms on his corduroy pants. "It was a few months ago when the carnival was over in Jackson. I went through one of them sideshows. You know, where they got all the freaks. While I was in there I saw a fruit jar, and in this fruit jar was a thing, half-baby and half-sheep. Lord God, to know that I might have fathered one of them, that it might have been mine."

"That's the most horrible thing I've ever heard of," said Carrie Ruth.

"Billy Roy, you've been worrying over nothing," said Parker. "That simply can't happen. There's no way biologically that a man and an animal can reproduce."

"How do you know, Parker?" asked Billy Roy.

"Did the thing look like you?" asked Carrie Ruth.

"Sis, will you shut up!"

"It's a hoax, Billy Roy, a lie. All unborns look like little babies when they're in the embryo stage. Somebody just found a miscarriage from a sheep and put it in a jar for gullible people to come along and think it's real."

"It was real, Parker. You should have seen it. I dream about it at night. God won't never forgive me for what I've done. To think I've fathered one of those things."

"There's no forgiveness needed from God for this because you didn't do anything."

"What about you, Carrie Ruth? Will you forgive me?"

"I don't know, Billy Roy; this is just so much to comprehend right now."

"See, I told you it was awful." Like a rocket, Billy Roy jumped to his feet and ran out of the house yelling, "I can't live with this on my mind!"

Carrie Ruth ran behind him crying, "It's OK, Billy Roy, it's OK." But Carrie Ruth's approval went unheard, for guilt deafens the ear of the confessor.

Later that evening the Bowman household received a phone call telling them that Billy Roy lay in a coma from a self-inflicted bullet wound to the head. Carrie Ruth backed up the day in her mind, but nothing changed. Life is not a Rook game; you can't throw back a day and ask to be dealt another.

October turned into Thanksgiving and the Bowmans tried to go on with their world. However, the turkey on the dining room table seemed to have more life. Not much was said at the meal with the exception of, "Pass the biscuits and mashed potatoes, please." That evening Henry Bowman found Parker in the front porch swing. Henry walked over to his favorite old rocker. He knew Parker was not himself, and he knew the front porch was the best psychiatrist in the world.

"What's wrong, son?"

"I don't know, Daddy. Somehow I just don't fit anymore. I've always loved my home, you, Carrie Ruth, and mama, but I can't talk with them like I used to. It's not only my family, but my friends, too. Billy Roy is lying in a room like a vegetable for the rest of his life 'cause of a ten-cent lie in a Ball fruit jar. Carrie Ruth is planning a future over a Fourth of July cakewalk. Mama stares at a funeral home calendar and counts the days so she won't have to face today. This place is beginning to suffocate me; it protects and keeps out anything that is not desirable. Reality doesn't live here."

Henry leaned forward in his old rocker. "There's a name for what you're feeling, son; it's called 'growing pains.'"

"Good grief, Daddy, I've been grown for years."

"You're right, son. Carrie Ruth is a grown woman and so is your mama, but I'm talking about the growing after you're grown. That's what you're doing, and it's nothing against your sister or your mama. It's just our world is smaller than yours. You see, we're like the maple and the oak trees. For them there is a season, like you read in the Bible. Every year we know that winter comes and spring will follow. Just like the trees in our yard, we all shed our leaves and color, and like them, we'll look like gray skeletons reaching toward our God. Next spring the maple and oak will come back, and they will come back in the same shape and color that they left. But you, son, are an evergreen. An evergreen knows no season; it's alive all the time, and it's always growing. And it continues to grow until it's cut down by life. Even at Christmastime we bring it in, and we decorate the evergreen because it's still alive in December, and even after it's cut down, it struggles to live. We stand and watch while it dies a long death in our living room."

"Is that what I am, Daddy, an evergreen?"

"Yes, son. An evergreen might need trimming back now and then when it gets out of shape, but the main thing is that it continues to grow. You'll leave us, son, your family, your friends, your home, but that don't mean you don't love us. You've just outgrown us. You've got to feed your mind. It can't grow without the food of knowledge. It don't mean that you won't come back on holidays or special occasions. You'll always come back because this is where your roots are planted. Even the evergreen comes back to its roots."

"Were you ever an evergreen, Daddy?"

"I nearly was once, but I wasn't strong enough to endure the winters. But I did go to the moon one time."

"What'd you find there?"

"I found that the man in the moon was me. But it wasn't what I found when I got there that mattered; it was the going that counted. Everyone's got a moon to go to. My moon was you, Carrie Ruth, your mama, this home. I wouldn't trade that for anyone else's moon, not even yours, son."

That night Parker went to bed and thought about what his father had told him.

Mary counted funeral home days until Christmas. Henry got his usual tie, and Parker got his usual knitted sweater. Parker gave Carrie Ruth a year's pass to the picture show, and Mary got the dress she had seen in the window at Lacy's Dress Shop. Parker planted a cedar outside of Billy Roy's window.

"Parker, why in this world would you plant a dumb old cedar outside Billy Roy's window? A maple has beautiful, colorful leaves in the fall. It would have been much prettier."

Henry walked over and put his arm around Carrie Ruth. "Don't bother your brother, Carrie Ruth; it's bedtime. I've got a feeling tomorrow the wind is going to be out of the southeast."

The next day the southeast wind blew along the Greyhound that took Parker away from home and loved ones. On the outskirts of town, as the bus passed the city limit sign, he smiled and looked back at his Yazoo City, a yazoo town.

Marshall McDuffy Learns a Lesson

The old No. 5 "NC and Saint L" stopped in Bell Buckle, Tennessee, long enough to let off a young man who had been contracted to teach at the local elementary school.

Emily Finney had taught science at the school for over fifty years but had died of pneumonia after falling on the ice and breaking her hip that winter. This left a teacher's position, and the school was very excited to get Marshall McDuffy, who had graduated from one of those good Virginia colleges. Not only did he have a background in science, but he had acting experience, and the elementary school needed a director for school plays. Marshall thought he was stepping back in time when he stepped off the train. Bell Buckle to him seemed like a small western town he'd seen so many times in cowboy movies. The town was a half square shaped like an "L" turned backwards; the buildings, sporting names like Clary's Drugstore, Paty's General Store, and Claxton's Grocery, were joined by old red bricks with thick walls. Marshall knew he would love this place because he loved small towns and small-town people. He couldn't wait to start his new job.

His first mission was to find where Bessie Turnbull lived. The principal had made arrangements for him to rent an upstairs bedroom in Miss Bessie's large, yellow Victorian house which was set among white dogwoods and pin oaks. Miss Bessie was an old maid of seventy-eight who sat on the veranda talking and answering herself, dressed in a merry widow which she wore on the outside of her clothes. People in Bell Buckle never quite knew if she were eccentric or touched, but to the locals they meant the same thing.

Marshall noticed a young boy roller skating and stopped him to ask directions to Miss Bessie Turnbull's house. The boy answered, "Are you sure you want to go there?"

Marshall wrinkled his brow and wondered what the child

meant by that. The youngster pointed his finger and said, "Go down about three blocks and turn right at the big tree; then go one block and turn left at the fencepost; then go two blocks and turn left at the telephone pole; then count four houses on the right. You can't miss her: she'll be the one in her underwear talking to herself."

Wondering what he was in for, Marshall picked up his suitcase and walked toward the tree, fencepost, and telephone pole. As he approached the yellow house, he heard Miss Bessie saying, "Isn't it a pretty day? Then again, it may rain. We need rain, but we don't need too much because we've had too much but not enough."

Marshall knew she wasn't talking to him, but he figured he must have been at the right house because there wasn't anybody else around talking to herself and wearing a corset. As he walked up the steps, he extended his hand and said, "I'm Marshall McDuffy, the new schoolteacher, and I believe you have a room reserved for me."

Miss Bessie, a little annoyed that he had interrupted her conversation, got up from her wicker rocker and mumbled, "Glad to meet you, young man. Your room is at the top of the stairs on the left, but I could put you at the right on the bottom of the stairs, except that in that room the sun comes in early and would wake you up. But then again, you need to wake up early if you're going to be teaching school. But maybe it doesn't matter since it rains most of the time anyway."

"Do you sleep upstairs or downstairs, Miss Bessie?"

"Well, sometimes I sleep upstairs when I take a notion, but then I don't like to climb the stairs, so I sleep downstairs most of the time. Except I should sleep upstairs because I need to climb the stairs for exercise, but too much exercise makes my joints hurt. So I sleep wherever my joints tell me."

Marshall wasn't sure where to sleep, but he picked the upstairs bedroom, hoping her joints wouldn't choose the room next to him too often.

"You just go on up yonder and make yourself at home. The bath is on the left, unless you want to use the one on the right, but the one on the left has a shower and the one on the right has a tub. The one on the left has an electrical outlet near the sink, but the one on the right is such a pretty green."

Marshall climbed the stairs confused and wondered what kind of a mess he'd gotten himself into. He avoided more of Miss Bessie that night by retiring early.

The next morning Miss Bessie took forty-five minutes to decide whether she should cook biscuits or have cornflakes with half a banana. But then what was she going to do with the left-over banana half since Marshall had told her he didn't like bananas? She liked the new brand of cornflakes because they had a full day's supply of vitamins, but she ended up eating an English muffin with jelly. Marshall said he'd just have one of the biscuits the principal had said were so good at the schoolhouse.

Except for his encounters with Miss Bessie, Marshall's first week in Bell Buckle was rather uneventful. However, a couple of weeks later when he was teaching science classes and directing plays after school, he faced the most confusion he'd seen in his lifetime. Billy Ray Riddle, a fifth grader in his fourth-period science class, had gone home one afternoon to help his father deliver a calf that was in trouble. Billy Ray was used to pulling calves, and his daddy had promised him he could have this one. The boy watched his calf being born and talked to his daddy about the new school year.

"Whatcha learnin' in school now, son, and how you like that new science teacher?"

"I really like him, Daddy; I'm learning a lot. Did you know I'm a homo sapien?"

Billy Ray's daddy looked at his son and said, "A what?"

"A homo sapien."

"A homo sapien? What kinda learnin' is goin' on in that

school?"

"Aw, Daddy, it's just part of being human."

"No son of mine is gonna be no homo sapien! I'm calling that schoolhouse right now and talk to that new teacher."

"Well, what you gonna talk to him about, Daddy?"

"I'm gonna talk to him about this homo stuff. The very idea of talkin' like that in the classroom and tellin' my son he's one. I don't want you or your sister Ila Mae bein' around the likes of him."

"But Daddy, Ila Mae loves acting in those plays he directs after school. Why, he even said she's gonna be a promising thespian."

"A what?"

"A thespian, Daddy. Why, she might even go to New York where them famous thespians are."

Henry Riddle threw off his calf delivering gloves and said, "That's it. We're goin' to that schoolhouse right now."

"But, Daddy . . ."

"Don't 'But' me, son. Git in that pickup truck. We gonna have a face to face talk with that new teacher."

Henry and Billy Ray arrived at the school just as play rehearsal was ending. Henry found Marshall in the principal's office, where he was picking up his afternoon mail. When the principal, Mr. Huffman, saw the father and son approaching his door, he rose to shake Henry Riddle's hand. "Hi, Henry. I'd like you to meet our new science teacher, Marshall McDuffy."

"That's what I'm here for: to talk about this here new science teacher. My son came home today and told me Mr. McDuffy said he was a homo sapien and his sister was probably gonna be a thespian."

Mr. Huffman looked at Henry and said, "What's wrong with that?"

"What's wrong with that? What's wrong with that? What kinda learnin' is goin' on here? The very idea he'd call younguns such a horrible thing. What's this world comin' to? There ain't no way Billy Ray is no homo and his sister ain't no thespian neither."

Marshall knew he needed to get in on this conversation. "Mr. Riddle, I think you've misconstrued what I said."

"I ain't misconscrewed nothin' and if you gonna use language like that you need to be in one of them towns in California where folks are turned that way."

Mr. Huffman turned to Henry and said, "I think you're misunderstanding what Marshall is saying."

Marshall interrupted the principal, and turning to Mr. Riddle, explained, "Sometimes words are difficult for people. For instance, there's the old story about the church that didn't have much light, and one of the members passed away, leaving money to improve the church so people could see better. A committee went out and came back with a report that they'd found a large chandelier. One of the members said, 'We don't need a chandelier; it costs too much money, and besides, nobody would know how to play one. What we need is more light.'"

Henry Riddle shook his head in disbelief. "What in the world has a story about V.D. in some church got to do with this?"

"V.D.?" said Marshall bewildered.

"What kinda church do you go to, anyway? One of them newfangled churches where anything goes?"

"Mr. Riddle, you're just really confused. I'm not teaching your son or daughter anything bad. I'd be glad to go over my syllabus with you anytime."

"Your syllabus? First the church has got it and now you done caught it. Harry Huffman, what kinda school you runnin' here?"

"Now, Henry, I'm running the same kind of school that I've always run. I'm afraid there's just been a misunderstanding, and I know it can be cleared up in time. Why don't you and Billy Ray meet with Harriet Clower, the guidance counselor, and we'll get this all straightened out tomorrow."

"Well, we better get it straightened out or my younguns ain't comin' here no more."

Henry Riddle put his arm around Billy Ray and said, "Come on, son." Then turning to Marshall, he asked, "Boy, where in the world you from?"

Marshall smiled and said, "Why, I came out of Wingina, a place in Virginia."

"Yer mama's got a pretty name, but round here we don't talk about our mamas' privates."

Marshall shook his head in disbelief as Henry and Billy Ray left the office. Mr. Huffman assured him everything would be OK and suggested he go home and have a good night's rest. As Marshall approached his front porch, he heard Miss Bessie saying, "I need to go to the bank and put my money in, but then if I put my money in the bank I might need money, and then I'd have to go to the bank and get my money out."

Marshall wished the train had never stopped in Bell Buckle.

The Cadaver

Cadavers were hard to find around the turn of the century. Graves were being robbed by young medical students, so rich folks hired someone to guard their newly buried loved ones. Coy Petty, a med student at the old Nashville College, didn't know what to do. He needed a cadaver.

His father, Amos, who lived in Bell Buckle, told him not to worry. He had a plan. Most anytime, someone was being buried in the paupers' part of the old Nashville City Cemetery. No one watched over poor folks. Usually, there was no one even to notify. He told Coy all they had to do was watch the old cemetery. In the meantime, Amos, who was so proud of owning the first rubber-wheeled wagon in Bell Buckle, decided the only way to steal a body and not get caught was going to take some planning. Coy, who was home one weekend from school, noticed his father motioning him to come out on the front porch.

"I don't want your mama to hear us talking, son. We're going down to Warren's Men's Store and buy a good suit and hat."

Coy told his father he really didn't need a new suit and hat.

Amos said, "It's not for you, son, it's for your cadaver. If we used one of mine, your mama will want to know where it is, and I'm danged sure not going to wear a suit after some dead pauper's been in it."

Coy worried the next few days. If they got caught, they would really be in trouble. Amos had a friend in Nashville who was on the lookout for a newly dug pauper's grave. He was to get in touch with him as soon as he discovered one. It had to be a dead male; after all, it would not be right to dig up some poor woman, but a poor man, that was different. He probably needed to be dug up.

The message arrived one afternoon, and Amos got word to Coy to meet him in front of his school. There was one more important ingredient in this robbery. Liquor. If they were going to get a body home, they had to pretend he was all liquored up. Hours later, Amos picked up Coy, and they headed to paupers' field. They pulled a wagon and mule behind several clumps of trees, and Coy got the shovel. Nervously, Coy headed for the grave. The dirt was still loose, so it didn't take long to dig up the body.

"I think I've struck the old wooden coffin, Daddy. We need to hurry. I'm so afraid we're gonna get caught."

"No one's gonna get caught, son, if we keep our heads. Just lift the body out, and close the lid, and throw the dirt back into the hole."

Soon Amos and Coy were lifting the cadaver on to the wagon. "Quick, son, get this new suit on him and this fine hat on his head."

Coy rushed to dress the man, and soon they were pulling out of the old cemetery. They had been lucky that the moon gave enough light because a lantern might have been noticed. Coy looked at the bottle of whiskey his daddy had on the seat.

"Daddy, you shouldn't be drinking. We're in enough trouble as it is."

"It's not for me, son. Here, pour it on the man. Make him smell good and drunk. Besides, he smells awful now. Whiskey will do him good."

Coy and Amos had gotten a few miles down the road when a city officer stopped them. "You men headed home?" said the officer.

"Yessir," said Amos. "Me and my son brought our friend into town to celebrate his birthday."

The officer looked over at the man and said, "Looks like he celebrated pretty good."

"Yessir, officer, he's dead drunk. We're just trying to get him home before his wife has a fit. You know these womenfolk worry all the time, and she's gonna be plenty mad he's got himself in this shape.

The officer shined his light on the corpse. "He looks mighty pale, you think he's OK?"

"Oh, sure, he always gets stiff when he drinks."

"Well, get on home, men, and be careful."

Amos and Coy rode toward Bell Buckle.

"That was a close one, Daddy."

"Not to worry, son. Your daddy can handle anything."

As Coy and Amos rode toward Bell Buckle, they had little conversation. Mostly Coy talked about the body.

"Wonder who he was, Daddy?"

"I don't have any idea, son, probably some old bum."

"It seems strange, Daddy; here we are with a man we don't know. We don't know who he was, don't know what he did, don't know where he's from."

Amos looked over at Coy. "Well, we know where he's going. He's going to Bell Buckle and get embalmed, and then to your school. I'll tell you one thing, he's never been this dressed up in his life."

It was early morning when Coy and Amos pulled into the barn at their Bell Buckle home. "Smell those biscuits, son; your mama's cooking breakfast."

"Isn't she going to wonder where we've been all night?"

"Nope, I told her I was visiting a sick cousin in Nashville."

Amos pulled the wagon into the barn, and he and Coy walked up to the back door of the house. Coy's mama, Olivia, met them at the back door, said they were just in time for a good breakfast, and asked how the cousin was feeling.

"He's much better; I think it was a shot in the arm to see me."

After breakfast, Coy and Amos went to their rooms to rest a while since they had been up all night. About two hours into a deep sleep, they heard screaming in the yard and into the house. They both jumped up to find Olivia running through the house with her hands in the air and yelling, "Oh, my God, oh, my God, there's a dead man in the barn!" This is something Coy and

Amos had not counted on. Both were trying to do some fast thinking.

"What are you talking about, Olivia?" said Amos. "What dead man?"

"Out there, Amos, out in the barn. I found him when I went out to feed the chickens. He's on your wagon. How in the world did a dead man end up in our barn on your wagon?"

Amos scratched his head. "Oh, that dead man."

"That dead man! How many dead men are around here?"

"Now, Olivia, don't get excited. It's actually my cousin; I just didn't want you to know he died. I thought it might upset you."

"Good grief, Amos, why didn't you just tell me the truth, and why in the world have you brought him back here?"

"Coy and I brought him home to be buried in the family plot. He didn't want a funeral; he just wanted to be dressed up in his finest suit and hat, and be put in the ground next to relatives. We're taking him down to the funeral home to be embalmed. I guess we should have told you when we got in, but we were just so tired."

Amos put his arm around Coy. "Let's get this body to the funeral home and go dig a grave in the cemetery."

Coy and Amos walked out to the barn. "How we gonna get out of this, Daddy?"

"We'll just dig a grave, put up a headstone, and pretend we buried my cousin. Your mama can bring him flowers and visit his grave when she feels like it. Everything will be all right. And when you're through with this cadaver, we'll bury him sure enough with the headstone."

Coy smiled and looked at Amos. "Well, at least now this man's got family."

Guitar, banjo and fiddle strings tied people together and pulled them toward the Mother Church of Country Music. Music was a refuge to those who worked in coal mines, factories, farm fields, and behind screen doors that led to newsprint papered walls. Pennies saved in fruit jars lined copper roads that led to the big auditorium where poor people sat and young children slept on old tabernacle oak pews that harmonized with rich mahogany. Music, seasoned with timbers from old Cumberland riverboats, brought magic to people looking for a rabbit's foot to make life easier. They came by train, bus, horse, car, truck, wagon and on foot. A red velvet curtain lifted blue hearts, and people with stars in their eyes heard music that told stories–their stories. And it happened in Nashville, Tennessee, in a place called the Ryman.

Let Her Go, Boys

You could set your clock by Tilly Mae Mingle. She got up at five every morning, took in washing and ironing for a living, and went to bed at eight every night. That is, every night but Saturday night. On Saturday she moved her bedtime to midnight. That night she sat up late, 'cause all she had to do on Sunday was go to church. However, Saturday nights were reserved for the Mother Church of Country Music, a large red brick tabernacle that sat on Fifth Avenue in Nashville, Tennessee. The Grand Ole Opry had become a Saturday night ritual of Tilly's. That was the time she set aside for herself. Her husband was killed in a coal mine accident in 1933, leaving Tilly to raise their three boys. Life was hard in Salyersville, Kentucky. Most men mined to make a living and many died of black lung. That's why Tilly wanted more for her boys. She was determined that her children would get a high school education, and her determination paid off. All of her boys finished high school, and two of them went on to college. With the boys grown and gone, life became a little easier, but now Tilly was getting up in years.

Tilly had another dream she had not fulfilled. She had spent her life listening to the Opry and dreamed of going there one day in person. Now the Opry was reaching a milestone. It was leaving the Ryman Auditorium to make its new home in a brand new building located on Briley Parkway in Nashville. Tilly didn't know where Briley Parkway was located, but she sure knew that old Ryman was near the corner of Fifth and Broad. Several of her friends had been there and had brought her back souvenirs of the old building. A picture of the Ryman stood in an antique frame that had been her mother's. As a matter of fact, a picture of Jesus had been covered up when the old Opry building went in that frame. Tilly would laugh when she passed the picture and would tell Jesus He was being held hostage until the day she could see the Opry in person. Besides, there was another picture of Him in the kitchen. After all, it wouldn't be a kitchen unless you had the Last Supper hanging near the kitchen table.

Now the Ryman had gotten too old and run down to be of much use. Tilly knew what the old building was going through. She, too, had gotten older and had outlived her usefulness. Her arthritic fingers could no longer do the nice ironing she once did. Her boys were grown and no longer really needed her. Life for her was just marking time.

Tilly had read in the paper that on March 9th the last Saturday night broadcast of the Grand Ole Opry from the Ryman was to take place. She had to be there. For thirty years the Opry had boomed out from that old auditorium to her living room. She remembered how the Opry announcer, the Solemn Old Judge, used to blow the deep boat whistle, and say, "Let her go, boys."

Soon, they would be saying that about the old building that was her Saturday night home away from home. She would sit in her old rocking chair crocheting and singing along with all the Opry stars. Minnie Pearl and Roy Acuff were her favorites. She even wrote Minnie one time, and Minnie answered back with a note telling Tilly how much she enjoyed her letter. Tilly kept that letter between Psalms in her Bible. She figured the songs of country music had just as much to say as the Psalms of David. Really, she had more in common with songs coming from that old Philco radio than she did with those in the Bible. Tilly was a woman of prayer, but she knew the Lord needed for her to help out any way she could; that's why she saved at least a penny a day in an old Mason fruit jar for all those years. Her kitchen cupboard was lined with copper. Copper jars were stored among green beans, red tomatoes, yellow corn, and purple beets; these vegetables Tilly had picked from her small garden and canned for winter, but the copper pennies were food for her soul. Her boys used to laugh and say that mama had more wheat on pennies than most farmers had in their fields.

With the boys out of the house, the walls echoed even more the sound of loneliness. Now and then they would bring her grandchildren for a visit, but they had their own lives, and grandmamas weren't really needed except on holidays. Through the years, country music offered even more comfort to Tilly. Hardships and loneliness were a way of life, and Opry singers made her feel like family. From that old Ryman stage stars had shared their lives in songs and stories. When songs were performed about coal mines and hard times, Tilly knew they were talking straight to her heart.

She knew that she had to make arrangements for the trip. She figured she'd saved enough for most of what she needed to do. There was the bus ticket, Opry ticket, and lodging. She had received a letter years before from her older first cousin, Beulah Atkins, who lived near Nashville in Bell Buckle, Tennessee, inviting her to come visit. They had only met once when Tilly was a little girl and Beulah had come to Kentucky for her and Tilly's grandmama's funeral. Beulah had stayed with Tilly's parents, and while she was there she taught Tilly how to make the best biscuits. But Beulah had passed away, and she had not kept up with her family. This meant Tilly would have to find lodging elsewhere. Friends had told her about the Hermitage Hotel near the Ryman. They also told her that she must go out to the Hermitage, home of Andrew Jackson, but it was Stonewall

Jackson that Tilly wanted to see. Stonewall had just showed up at the Opry and asked if he could sing his song. They let him sing; that's the kind of people they were.

It took Tilly several months to work out the arrangements. The Greyhound bus did not leave early enough to get her into Nashville in time for the show, so that meant two nights in the hotel. The roundtrip ticket, hotel room and Opry ticket came to ninety-six dollars and seventy-two cents. She ordered a flowered print dress from the Sears and Roebuck catalog to wear on that special Saturday night. The flowered dress in the catalog reminded Tilly of the song "Wildwood Flowers" that Maybelle Carter sang through the years. Each Mason jar held around ten dollars and thirty-four cents. This left Tilly thirty dollars and thirty-eight cents to eat on and maybe buy herself a little souvenir.

Tilly only had one problem. Her boys knew that she had been saving her pennies through the years to go to the Opry, but they never dreamed she'd really go to Nashville. Now, at sixty-nine years of age, she was to journey out of Salyersville for the first time in her life. The boys were dead set against this. On Sunday, the week before she was to leave, each of them came to her house to talk her out of the trip.

Tilly loved her boys but often wished she had a daughter she could talk to. Years before, Tilly lost her only chance when a daughter came stillborn. Now and then Tilly would look over to the old pine bed and remember the night she labored and how the Opry was playing during the delivery. Roy Acuff was singing "Precious Jewel." She could still hear those words, "A jewel here on earth, a jewel up in heaven." Tilly named her daughter Jewel that night, and the next morning buried her, wrapped in the flower-garden quilt her grandmama had given her when she was a little girl. Tilly's father had made a doll's cedar chest for her eighth birthday. Little did Tilly know that the chest she played with would become a small wooden coffin for her daughter. Maybe, had she lived, she would have understood Tilly's dream.

"Mama, you can't go off by yourself to Nashville, Tennessee. Why, you've never been much anywhere outside of this town, and I can't take off of work to take you myself."

"Don't worry about me, son. Nashville's just a big old country town, and I'm staying a few blocks from the Ryman. I'll be all right."

Her oldest boy suggested that she wait until summer and maybe the whole family could go.

"I ain't gonna wait till summer; it'll be too late. I want to see the Opry before it leaves the Ryman."

"Good grief, Mama, you've been sitting by that old radio all your life; looks like you'd have your fill of that old Opry by now."

"Boy, I'm filled with a lot of things. I'm filled up to my throat with tears that I've held in 'cause I didn't want you to see me crying; I'm filled up to my heart with aches that I stored through the years 'cause I didn't have time to fret. I'm up to my knees in blood from my feet walking on broken dreams. I'm filled up to my waist with things I'll never do, but I'll never fill up with the Grand Ole Opry. All those years. The Solemn Old Judge started that Opry with 'Let her go, boys.' If he were here right now, he'd be saying that to y'all. Now I've checked on everything. The bus carries me near my hotel, and the Ryman is only a few blocks from there. I may not have traveled to those big fancy towns like all of you, but I sure got sense enough to find my way around a few blocks. I got a cupboard full of cents in fruit jars, and I'm going. Nothing's gonna stop me unless the good Lord strikes me dead, and I'm feeling pretty good."

She was determined, and her boys knew what determination meant to their mama. They were still shaking their heads when they left, and Tilly was still shaking her finger.

The next few days seemed like eternity; Tilly could hardly sleep. In the weeks before, she had rolled her pennies and taken them to the bank. Sally Jacobs had turned them into cashier's checks and sent them to the appropriate places in Nashville. Everything was taken care of down to the last penny. All she had to do was pack her suitcase and get on the bus. Ida Bell took her to the bus station and sent her off with two sausage biscuits for her long bus ride. The ride to Nashville was a real treat. Tilly saw towns and cities she'd never seen. In every town station someone was getting off or getting on. They were strangers, yet she felt like they had a common bond. Perhaps they were going to the same place; after all, this certainly was a moment in Opry history. She talked to several of the passengers, but they were going other places–perhaps places they had dreamed about. It was several hours after dark when the bus pulled into the Nashville station. She asked for directions to the hotel, and a friendly ticket agent told her to go down two blocks and turn right. The hotel would be on her left. The March air in Nashville was nippy, but when Tilly looked up and saw that large red auditorium protruding above the surrounding buildings a warm feeling came over her entire body. Tilly couldn't take her eyes off it. The only time she looked down was when she passed a beggar on the corner of Sixth and Church Street. She laid a one dollar bill in his crumpled old dirty hat and walked on. She really didn't have money to spare, but she figured anyone down on his luck needed help, for who knows what that man's dreams might have been.

Soon the Hermitage Hotel came into view. It was a tall brick building full of windows. She wondered what window she would be looking out and if she could see the auditorium from her room. The heavy large doors opened into a spacious lobby with lots of brass and columns. Tilly had never seen so much brass, and the columns looked like pictures of Greek temples she had seen in magazines.

A short, round-faced man sat behind a large walnut counter. At first she didn't see him, but he rose to greet her. She asked for a room that might overlook the Ryman. The man told her that she would probably only see its roof and suggested she might want a room overlooking the Capitol. He went on to tell her a little history about the Capitol building and that it sat high on the hillside and was a beautiful sight at night. Tilly chose the view of the Ryman's roof. A bellman dressed in green and gray escorted her to the elevator. It was so shiny you could see your reflection in the door. Tilly wondered who in the world polished all that brass.

It was a short walk down a long corridor, and Tilly was glad to see her room and double bed. She unpacked the old cream and brown striped suitcase that one of her boys had used in college. It had been kept in the cupboard with the pennies. She hand pressed her wrinkled print dress and hung it in the small closet, then called her oldest son to tell him she had arrived all right and asked him to call the others. After hanging up the phone, Tilly walked over and pulled back the shade and looked out onto the bright lights of the city. For the first time she got a little uneasy. She wondered what kind of world was out there. It was a far cry from the world from which she came. She went to bed as excited as a child going to sleep on Christmas Eve. She wanted Santa Claus to hurry and get there.

Saturday morning she awoke with the daylight. Even though she was extremely tired when she went to bed, she did not sleep well. It was a strange town, a strange place and, most of all, a strange bed. The mattress was hard compared to the featherbed she had at home. She had saved one of Ida's sausage biscuits in her purse. The whole time she was eating it she thought about the beggar and wished she had given it to him. She was just so busy looking around she had forgotten she had it. She had been told not to eat at the hotel. Food in hotels was much more expensive than in other places.

She could see Harvey's department store from her window. She knew about Harvey's from commercials on the Grand Ole Opry, advertising it was the largest store in the central south. Tilly put on her housedress and crossed the street to the large department store. She couldn't believe its size. There were floors and floors of merchandise. What was harder to believe was that the store had been downsized through the years. However, the thing that fascinated her the most was the escalator. She had never seen moving stairs. At first she was afraid to get on them, for fear she would fall. She clutched the long black moving bar and finally got her feet on the step. It was the basement that Tilly really loved. Everything in there was marked down. She bought a pair of socks, a scarf, and a picture frame that looked a lot like the old one she had at home. She had lunch at the basement counter and returned to her room. She tried to nap awhile since she had not slept much the night before. However, she only rested because traffic kept her awake. She had never heard so many horns, and every time a siren went by she wondered if the hotel was on fire. The rest of the afternoon was spent looking out the window.

As night fell, Tilly rose to the occasion of getting dressed. She had pampered herself with a takeout chicken sandwich from Harvey's and had eaten it while soaking in the large bathtub in her room. She carefully removed her dress from the wooden hanger and slipped it over her head. Then she put on a little powder and lipstick. Soon she was on her way down Sixth Avenue toward Fifth. As she approached the Ryman, she saw a large crowd standing in line. Tilly went to the back and stood with the rest. Standing in line was like being in a daze, kind of like at her mama's funeral. Only there were no flowers, just the sweet smell of perfume on women who were dressed all kinds of ways. The next thing she remembered was a girl taking her ticket and pointing to a pew. Tilly had gotten a good seat near the front of the stage. She wondered who had sat in her pew through the years. Did they have the same dream? She took it all in: the walls, the windows, the balcony, the large pillars that supported the high ceiling. She knew about Tom Ryman, a riverboat captain who got religion one night when he heard Sam Jones preach. Tom wanted to build Sam a place to hold revivals, so he built the old tabernacle out of timbers from his riverboats. That's why the rich sounds of the Opry bounced off the walls.

Finally the time arrived. The red velvet curtain lifted and the show began. "From the great Atlantic Ocean, to the wide Pacific shore": Roy Acuff was singing the song he opened with each Saturday night. He was twirling his fiddle bow in one hand and balancing it on his nose with the other. One by one she saw them all as they came to the microphone and sang the first songs they had ever sung from the Ryman stage. Finally Minnie Pearl came on with, "Howdee, I'm just so proud to be here."

Tilly had waited for this moment. It was a voice that she had heard so many times. She thought of the letter from Minnie that she had back home. Then something special happened. Right in the middle of her routine, Minnie looked out at the audience and straight at her. It was like Minnie knew she was there. A warm feeling rushed over Tilly. It was like a spiritual experience. No one would believe her when she told this, but she believed it and that's all that mattered. The night went by like the Wabash Cannonball coming down the track. The last song was about to be sung, "Will The Circle Be Unbroken?" Everybody came out on the stage to sing. Tilly thought about loved ones that had gone on before and those Sunday singings in church, but the circle she thought about most was the circle that had been cut out of the Ryman stage and placed onto the stage at the new Opry House. They were taking part of the Ryman with them. The soul of the old girl was staying, but they were taking the heart. Before she left, she could hear the ghost of the Solemn Old Judge saying, "Let her go, boys," but tonight they were talking about the Ryman. She just couldn't keep up with the new Opry House. It was going to seat more, have air conditioning and be a lot more comfortable, but there was something she had in common with the old Ryman, and that was character. Tilly walked back to her hotel holding the precious program that she had bought the frame for. She now could go home and let Jesus, knocking at the door, in.

About The Author

Margaret (Maggi) Britton Vaughn is Poet Laureate of Tennessee. She is the author of five volumes of poetry and resides in Bell Buckle, Tennessee.